A H

Tale

A

Lola Bandz

Novella

A Hood Luv Tale : A Novella

Cover Design: Brittani Williams

Other Books By Lola Bandz

Fyast Life

Deranged Loverz

Diamond & Dolce Outlaws

Down A$$ Bitch

Tattered Hearts & Bruised Egos

Luving A Thug Series(1-3)

Baddest Of Them All

Hell On Heelz

Every Girl Needs A Thug Series

Don Divas

Dreams Of A D-Boy

Coming Soon

Dope Girlz Inc

Cali's Queen Pin

Illusion of the Hustle

Black Barbie

Bow Tiez & Banglez

Deranged Loverz 2

Diamond & Dolce Outlaws

Run: Kami & Gram

Baddest Of Them All

Me & My G

Similar Strangers

Save Me From You

Cocaine Cowgirlz Series (Also Known As Don Divas)

Contact Lola Bandz
Facebook : Lola Bandz
*Instagram: Lola_bandz_*
Twitter: Lola_Bandz
Email: Lolabandzz@gmail.com
www.dopegirllola.com[1]

Aspiring Authors

Rebellious Reign is accepting authors. Please submit the first 3 chapter along with contact information to: rebelliousreignproductions@gmail.com
Good luck

1. http://www.dopegirllola.com

Intro

Fairy Tales will never break when their real...

Paige

"I swear let this nigga not answer this fucking phone," I slammed onto the brakes as I swerved with Kita in the passenger side. She looked at me and shook her head. If anyone knew how me and Josiah were it was her. She knew that this nigga had my mind gone and heart open. It had been this way since I was in the 5th grade but back then I was too afraid to show it. Now here we were grown and sexy and living through some of the realest shit ever.

"But don't kill me in the process bitch," Kita said to me as I whipped the Pink G-Wagon into the driveway and rushed out. I pulled up to her house and saw that this niggas car was parked there and to say I was steaming was an understatement.

"I don't know who the fuck he thinks I am," I said to her as I power walked to the door and tried to open it but it was locked so I slammed on that hoe heavily.

Kita shook her head as she went into her purse and pulled her keys out and I chuckled a bit. I forgot she lived here. As soon as the door turned Josiah's sexy ass stepped out and looked at me. I rolled my eyes and looked down at his red bottom sneakers that I brought him as an early birthday gift last week, rag and bones jeans and black v-neck that he owned to a tee.

Fuck I loved this nigga and his deep waves helped none. I stood with my hands on my hips and he shook his head and bit his lips taking in my thick frame. My baby knew I owned this shit and his heart.

"Girl why you so fucking mad?" he questioned me and I looked away. I couldn't explain to him why I was so fucking mad. Shit he was sexy that's why. I loved his sexy ass and his hoe ass ways didn't ease my heart. Even though he swore up and down that he never fucked a bitch while I was around I knew it was a lie. A nigga will tell you the sky is purple, just to mend your heart, and a dumb ass woman will eat it up. He grabbed me into his embrace and kissed my cheek and then began to fondle the ass he couldn't stop grasping. I giggled and looked for Kita but her ass was gone.

"I called you and texted your ass," I hit his arm while he eased me back to the truck.

"I aint get shit ma," he said kissing me more and easing his hands into my pants and then unbuckled them. I looked around, it was 2 pm and he was outside trying to get some ass, the worse part was I was going to give it to him.

"Daddy stop lying," I moaned as he lifted my leg out of my jeans and spread me across the hood.

"Fuck I gotta lie for P? what daddy say about trusting him?" he said planting one finger deep in my dripping wet tunnel and then plunged into my wet walls deep, I gasped from the girth of him. He knew I couldn't take it when he did that. I felt that shit hit my guts.

"I...I," I stuttered shit that's all I could do. He opened my legs wider and began to pound my insides out.

"Ya' nigga gets this pussy don't he?"

"Yessss," I moaned as he pinched my nipples and grinded into me.

"Then why you questioning a nigga, the way I give you dick I can't afford to have another bitch," he said closing his eyes as I clamped my pussy muscles down on him.

I don't know why I questioned my man, maybe because we were too perfect. After a minute he nutted off in me and then pulled me in close for a kiss. One thing I had to say about Josiah is that he didn't give a fuck who was watching, when he wanted his kitten to purr he made that hoe meow. Fixing me up and smacking my ass he shook he head as I tried to switch in the house.

"You know damn well this dick can't have you walking normal, you still aint used to it," he said and I laughed. He was right though. I looked at him and loved the man that he was. He took me on extravagant trips, nightly chef made dinners, I got whatever I needed and didn't need shit else. I guess I just needed to trust in my man.

"I love you Paige," he said to me in a genuine tone and it touched my heart.

"I love you more," I blew him a kiss and watched him walk to his car, a black with white interior 1979 mustang and roll the windows down.

"Dinner at 8 baby?" I nodded. Yup I loved Josiah and nothing would ever stop that. And I'm a warn you now if you don't like mushy love stories that's good because this isn't the way that we started but it's the perfect love story for me, so cliché.

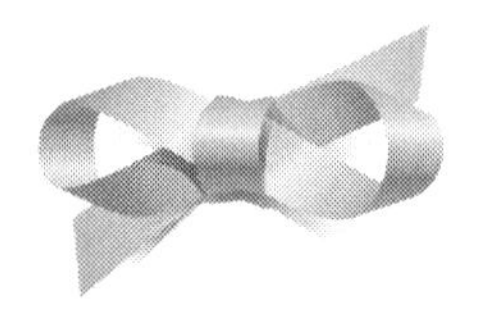

1
Love & Happiness

"Ahhh hell no, yall cheating." Anna Walton said to her family as they all sat around the small table playing the board game "Sorry," It was fit perfectly well for them. It had four pieces for the four of them in their family. The red one was always claimed by Paige her daughter and green was claimed by Daryl, leaving her and her husband with yellow and blue. That was always fine by them.

"You always talking bout someone cheating ma' get on somewhere." Daryl laughed as he watched his mother pout.

"Yall do." She giggled followed by her 16-year-old daughter.

"Mama stop; you know we don't." Paige laughed.

"Whatever forget yall I gotta turn the fish anyhow." Anna smiled as she got up and her husband looked her over and yelled out break. The kids smiled grabbing their cells to check in with their friends with the latest text as Avon got up to go and check on his wife.

The Walton family was cut from a different clothe in the year of 2006. They kept family values alive and well and they very much depended on one another for stability. Avon made sure of that when he was a youngsta' he always told his mother that he would have a wife, with a boy and a girl. He would have a big house and raise his family right, and that he did. He made sure to be the dad that his very own father lacked to be.

Walking into the kitchen he looked around and the cheery yellow sunshine's that were plastered everywhere with the lord's word all throughout the kitchen, even the house. Anna was a firm believer in the man upstairs so she made sure that her family attended church, meetings, events, and studies on a regular.

"That girl think that she so fine... I gotta make her mine..." Avon, sang in her ear as he twirled her around and caught her just in time. She giggled and he felt as though an angel kissed his cheeks. She was so inviting and alluring that he knew he would be stuck with her forever, and he knew that since the moment he met her in college.

The two started off as college rivals but Avon knew all the while she would be his wife. That was a given and he was to make sure that she knew that.

"It's that she would have my mind baby." Anna giggled as she took the whiting out of the pan and placed it on the two white paper towels staining the paper towels with grease. Looking down at the golden fish Avon licked his lips and then stole a kiss from her.

"I promise you, I can't wait to eat some of that good food."

"What food?" she hinted with a smirk. Smacking her on the bottom he turned her away and walked out. He needed to get back to the kids in the living room before her got to carried away.

As soon as he walked out of the kitchen she smiled as Paige walked into the kitchen and began to set the table.

"Ma?" she started. Anna looked up into her daughter's beautiful brown eyes and smiled.

"Yes my love."

"Ummmm, do you think that I can ask you a question?"

She grabbed the plates and started to place them on the table along with the silverware. Anna made sure that no matter the cause they ate together. Her daughter and son deserved that.

"Yes baby." She said taking the broccoli out of the steamer and placing it into the serving bowls along with the yellow rice. Paige looked at the food and felt a hunger pang she hadn't ate all day and was waiting for it.

"I kinda like someone." She began and her mom dropped the serving spoon into the bowl startling Paige.

"Un huh?"

"And I was wondering, like what can I do to get him to look at me the way that daddy looks at you?"

Sighing Anna walked over to her and placed her hand on her shoulder.

"Baby, you are too young to date and worry about a boy. Make him your friend, that's why your daddy looks at me like that. He respects me and that's what you need. Never mess with a boy, always a man." She winked and turned to continue making her dinner.

Paige smiled and finished setting the table.

On the inside, Anna was boiling over with excitement and nerves. Her baby was starting to look at boys and she couldn't wait for the day to become a grandmother. She knew that it would be a while but just thinking about having a happy family filed with love she couldn't help but to wonder what the future had in store.

• • ❧ • •

"HI KITA," PAIGE SAID as her best friensd walked over to her as they stood in the hallway. Kita Brown and Din Martin were Paiges best friends and had been since preschool, they loved one

another so much and had one another's back that no one could come in between that.

"Ooowweee bitch you looking cute." Kita smiled at her best. Din smiled in agreement. She was so quiet at times around others but she was down just like her girls.

Paige was looking really cute in her levis, Nike air max, and a plain tee. Her hair was up in a donut bun and she wore her gold jewelry that she had gotten for Christmas, she was fly and anyone in Mt Eden high knew that.

"So why the hell Jerry text me last night." Paige said slamming her locker. Kita looked at her.

"What?" Kita excitedly said.

"Girl this is wassap, we can all have dates now." Din was so excited she could jump out her skin.

"No wipe those smiles off of yall face. I'm not talking to him like that." She blew her bubblegum and walked through the halls. They walked straight out of school and onto the blacktop where all the people they hung out with were.

Paige locked eyes with the guy that she had been feeling since 5th grade. Josiah "Flex" Foster. Once Kita saw him she rolled her eyes. Josiah was known to have all the groupies on his line, especially since he was one of the bay areas largest drug dealers little brother. He stayed fresh in the latest gear and he basically had his own crib. Being that he was 2 years older than Paige she wanted him more than anything.

"That nigga is so damn fioneeee." She stressed to her girls.

"Man that nigga aint all that best."

Kita let her known as they walked passed him as he eyds Paige. He had been watching her for a while and he loved how she carried herself. She never threw herself at a man, never made anyone feel lower than her since she had both of her parents. She was just really humble and sweet.

"Hi Paige." His best friend Trey waved and she smiled and waved back. In a way Josiah wanted to take her from his vision but he knew he would be tripping if her did that, and if it was one thing that Josiah Foster did it was never to trip off a girl.

"Girl see now Trey." Din said out loud not being able to hold in her liking for him.

"If you want Trey so bad, girl go and be with Trey." She threw at her and then walked over to their group of friends.

"Girl Trey and Josiah asses over there looking like Paid In Full ass niggas." Jahari a local girl from the school said while licking her lips. Jahari came from a different mindset than Paige, she did as she pleased and didn't care about throwing dirt on her parents name. She only had one anyway and that was her mom, who was too busy raising and running the streets over her two older sisters Jessica and Jasmine. They were both 17 and 16 and they loved to give her a run for her money.

Paige kept quiet as she over looked the boy that had skin as dark as night, nice lotion, healthy shine. Lance Gross skin that she just wanted to rub. His waved were dipping, and his swag was impeccable, he had that grown man appeal and he owned his sexiness.

"If daddy don't know he sexy I can take him off anyone's hands." Vanile the only white girl in their crew said.

They all looked at her and shook their heads.

"Nah Van I got this" Jahari smiled looking over at Paige.

Jahari knew that Paige had a crush on him, hell they all did, the only issue was that Jahari was fast and she wasn't going to wait on anyone to take her man, friend or family. She was going to go in for hers. Vanilla looked at Paige's face as Jahari went and sat next to the boys. She wore a look of disappointment as she saw a smile spread on Josiah's face. Walking up to her and rubbing her back she said so only she could hear.

"She's a hoe. That's easy pussy, I see how he stares at you. Don't worry sis you got 'em."

"Aye?"

"Aye!"

Someone yelled in Paige's face as she snapped back into reality and saw that she was at work in her Denny's Restaurant outfit. Rolling her eyes and looking away she looked back at him.

"What?" She asked as she stared at him in disbelief for yelling at her. Once she realized that it was her step sisters man she rolled her eyes.

"Bye Josiah your girlfriend is sitting right over there in the back with her ratchet ass friends." She rolled her eyes and went to the next customer.

Josiah clench his jaw and shook his head as much as he wanted to embarrass her for having an attitude with him he let it slide, she had always been that way with him but he was going to make her stop. Sliding his hand over his freshly cut goatee he fixated his pretty grey eyes on her.

"Don't get an attitude with me Paige I'm not the one you should be upset with." He walked off and she caught a glimpse of his sexiness. His cologne filled her nostrils and she knew exactly which it was because she went into Macys until she found the exact scent that lingered from him, the only difference was that his chemicals made the cologne smell that much better than the bottle.

Looking back at her he caught her staring and she looked away. Shaking his head as he smirked he joined the table with his two best friends, his girl, and her friends.

"Why the fuck you talking to her?" Jahari asked. They had been off and on fuck buddies for the past 4 years. He couldn't stand her mouth but her head game was A1. He felt like a sucka every time he tried to leave and she put her head game on him.

Vanilla looked at her and jerked her head back, not wanting to say anything but no longer being able to contain herself.

"Look bitch I'm bout tired of you and ya' shade. That's annoying." she pointed her pale pink nails at her and rolled her eyes. Vanilla was cool with both sisters so she didn't see the point in her going in on her every time she saw her.

"Girl bye I don't give a fuck how no one feel. This me, aint that right daddy?" she asked kissing his cheek and easing her hand down his jeans. He shook his head and smacked her hand away from him.

"You need to chill the fuck out." He said turning to his two childhood friends, Malik and Drizz, they were always and would always be his niggas. He loved them like brothers along with Trey. They had their own lil' crew and everyone knew them by the Billionaire Boyz.

"Where Trey at?" he asked Malik.

"Shit last I talked to him he was just landing." Malik pulled his iPhone out and texted him.

"Cool, when that nigga get here we need to link up."

"Asap." Drizz said looking at his date, which was Vanilla for the night.

Jahari looked at Vanilla and began to get agitated by the way that she was talking about Paige to Malik. She talked about her beauty, her hair, her spirit and her in general. She hated her with a passion and hoped that she knew that.

"V shut up bruh, I'm so tired of yall discussing her basic ass." Jahari said running her hands in her 22 inch hair. Josiah looked at her and shook his head. He was so tired of her antics.

"Man shut up, and stop running your hands through that ugly ass hair. That shit gonna get in my food and I'm a have to beat your ass." He joked but he held a serious tone. She stopped running her hands through her hair and rolled her eyes.

"Whatever, this bitch better hurry up with our order."

• • ❧ • •

IN THE BACK ROOM, PAIGE was crying her eyes out. She missed her family and the only thing that brought on joy for her was the memories that they shared 6 years ago before all the bullshit began.

"Paige?" Kita said knocking on the door. Paige jumped up in hopes that her best friend wouldn't see her crying the tears that she held in on a daily.

"You crying?" she asked her and she nodded. She couldn't hold it in any longer. She was tired of faking. She was tired of acting like her life was grand. Here she was 20 years old, living under her parent's roof and she was miserable.

She had nothing at the moment, no car, nothing. Even though she was attending Cal State east bay she was ready to give up. She was tired of faking and she was tired of praying because it seemed like all the people who were doing wrong were living great and here she was living horribly.

Kita walked over to her friend and pulled her in for a hug. Rubbing her back she made her give up the tears she had been holding in for so long.

"It's ok." Kita consoled her and continued to console her because she knew that she was lost right now. She knew her life wasn't right and she wished it all could go back to how it was 6 years ago.

Wiping her eyes and looking at her best friend she smiled and then straightened up.

"I'm good baby, let me go over here and make this money." She laughed and Kita snapped her fingers.

"That's the baby girl I know." She smiled and they grabbed their orders and went on about their night.

Working hard throughout the night and putting up with her sisters horrible attitude her shift was over and she and Kita were leaving out the door. She was happy it was over so she could go home, relax, and read a good book before having to study.

"Girl I wanna go out." Kita said moving her hips as they drove down the street listening to Drake's "Hotline Bling." Kita also was smoking, something that she loved to do and couldn't give up. And being from Oakland where the weed was so fire was a plus.

"No girl I'm not going out, I wanna curl up and chill." She said laughing at Kita and her pretty brown skin while she looked like 2Pac while smoking. Both girls were a beautiful shade of warm freshly baked cookies and that's why she loved her best friend, they were perfect in her eyes.

"Come on why not?"

"Cuz' Kita I'm tired; we been working all damn night." She stressed while looking in the mirror. Her hair was a mess and plus she had no clothes.

"Girl and?"

"Kitttaaaaaa I have no clothes and look at my hair."

"Bitch and?" she laughed as she turned the street to go to her house.

Looking over at her she shook her head. She knew Kita and she normally always got what she wanted. So she gave in and thought about it not one little night wont hurt.

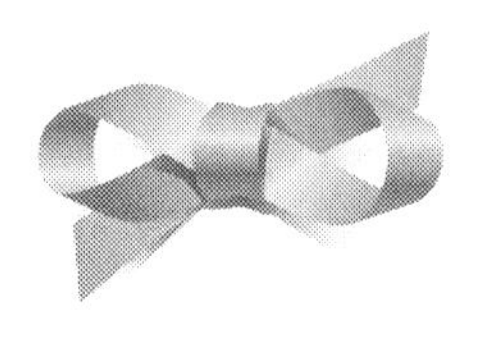

2
Happily, Never Again

"I love you baby," Avon said as they walked to the boat. Jannika smiled and shook her head at his fine ass. She had been blessed to be by his side through the death of his wife, help raise his children and love him. In the process she built herself a good man. She knew that he would never get over his first wife and that was ok because the love that she held for him and his million-dollar life insurance policy was all that she needed.

3 months prior Anna was killed by a marked gunman as she tried to help a man in a bank robbery while she was off duty. She loved saving lives and being an EMT was all she strived for so she risked her life trying to do right by this man. In the end the man survived but the gunshot to the head killed Anna instantly on the scene.

Avon, Daryl, and Paige were taking things bad, so bad that Daryl turned to drugs and he ran to a 37-year-old woman for comfort. Disobeying his dads wishes he moved out at the age of 17 and moved in with his suga mama. Leaving Paige and her dad to care for one another. Some nights life was great, some nights she forgot her mother was dead as well he. They both would wait for hours for Anna to come in, show that smile that they thrived on to survive, cook dinner and pray. But those nights never came.

Not being able to live like they were any longer Paige decided that she was ready to go back to the church and her dad followed. Staying there night and day and praying they found their salvation in the lord.

One day, at a church picnic, Jannika showed up with her three daughters. 14-year-old Jahari, 16-year-old Jessica, and 17-year-old Jazmine, Paige was so happy to see one of her friends from school that the befriendment went easy. Once Jannika and Avon met and she heard his story she just knew the good lord sent her to him and she didn't stop until she and her girls moved into their house, and was granted the world.

Avon was a man's man and he made sure that they were well taken care of and she loved him about that. The girls were spoiled, and Paige did everything to make them feel good at home, but one day they went on a trip to Aruba and he never returned. Jannika came back from the "baecation" with a sorrowed heart, and as Mrs. Avon Walton.

"There that bitch go right there mama." Jazmine said as she looked at Paige from her instagram page.

"Fuck that little bitch." She spat rolling up her weed as she propped her feet up on the 1,000 couch that she scammed from Rent-A-Center. Even though she was left with a nice hefty amount of change she blew through that quickly.

Ms. Jannika Stephenson was the meanest step mother that Paige could have been cursed with and she hated the ground that Paige walked on and even though it was her dad's savings that kept the bills afloat, food in her tummy, and her kids in good schools, she paid no respect and no mind to Paige. They all treated her as though she could have been Cinderella or even worse in a VC Andrews book "Flowers in The Attic."

"Mama why this lil' ass girl was talking hella shit to me when I went to her job and ordered my food?" Jahari said walking into the pink and gold themed living room. She was wearing a red bondage dress that left little to the imagination.

"What she say? And your lil' hoe ass looks cute." Jannika winked.

"Girl just talking bout she wants Josiah, how he was supposed to be hers, yadiyadiya."

Jahari lied as she walked throughout the living room giving them their freshly served tea built on lies and self hate. Looking at her mom she could see why any man would want her. Her pretty light skin, long weave, and beautiful features made her irresistible. The only issue was that Jannika was rotten to the core after her husband left her side. She turned all of her daughters into spoiled rotten girls as well.

As they all sat around and chopped up Paige, Jannika sat and thought of a way to try and take her out and away from them for good.

• • ❧ • •

"HEY MA." JOSIAH SPOKE to his mother Shantriece, she was a beautiful woman skin as rich and deep as coffee grounds, wide mothering hips and a plump shaped figure. Shantriece was a woman that was born and bred in Kingston Jamaica and anyone that knew her or met her knew that. She had a beautiful commanding spirit.

Growing up she never had a great life, so she made sure that Ghana-Keyair "Josiah" Foster wanted for nothing in life. She left Jamaica and his rude boy of a father when she was 4 months pregnant and never went back. There were times when his Dad wanted him and sent for him, which was fine by her even though she didn't approve of his gangster life she could never deny them their relationship. She looked at her son and was very happy of who he had became.

"Hey dere boy," she kissed his cheek as she sat on her imported Italian chaise. The Jamaican ganja that she only smoked laced the air leaving a sweet husky smell telling you it was freshly grown from a rasta man himself. He walked to the kitchen and thumbed through the letters that was there.

"Ma nothing for me?"

"Ya don't see nothing over dere duh yah now bway?" he shook his head and laughed as his mother was watching her soaps "Days Of Our Lives."

"You need some food or anything?"

"No stop your worrying about your mother boy. Me cook ya some supper, take it home from the fridge and eat it son." She assured him.

Going into the refrigerator he poked around until he found his three big Tupperware containers made especially for him. He loved when his mom cooked him food. He never had to go out and eat anywhere because she looked out for him. As he looked into the containers he saw that she made Oxtails, rice & beans, and rum cake. He smiled as he thought about digging in her food when he closed the door to the fridge he looked around at the 5-bedroom home that he brought for her two years ago and he loved how she had everything decorated to a tee.

She got up walking over to him and rubbed his back. She looked at her handsome son. She took in his chocolate skin, and 6 foot two frame. His deep waves, stone cold grey eyes, he looked like his fathers twin at the same age his father was. She knew that he gave all the women a run for his money.

"When are you going to give me a baby boy? Me not getting any younger ya know bway" she laughed as she saw his expression change. He shook his head and looked at his mother.

"I love you ma." He kissed he cheek and she saw him off.

"Ghana?!"

"Yea ma?"

"Me not playing with you ya hear me nuh? Me want grand kids, cute babies to run around and feed. Yuh 26 years old nuh bway. And get rid of that rotten girl, me don't trust her ya 'ere?" she spoke on Jahari. She never liked her and he knew that.

He nodded as he closed her door and jogged to his silver Coupe Mercedes Benz S class. He shook his head at his mother's antics. She was in her prime being a nice 44 years of age. She wanted grand kids to spoil and he didn't want to provide her with any. Especially how his life was at this moment, he lived with no regard for life and loved being young, wild, and free. As he curved the streets of San Francisco, he waited for the call that he had been waiting for all day. Work.

"Wassap?" he answered the phone as Jahari called him up.

"Baby where are you I miss you, we still going out?" He made a face that he wished he could see.

"Sure me and all the other niggas huh?" he told her as she thought he was going to fall into the thirst trap that she set up for all other niggas. Jahari and him had been on the rocks for a couple months, and after she told him that she was fucking one of his enemy's he didn't trust her as far as he could trust her, but he kept her around just for information that she might have had, but now he was seeing that maybe he didn't need any of it. He didn't want to get caught slipping fucking around with her.

"Anyway are you coming to the party tonight? Everyone will be looking for you, especially Trey," she spoke slighted with an attitude while changing the subject.

"Look don't worry about that. Did your mailman come and drop off my mail?"

"No not yet." She spoke truthfully and he believed her, no one would dare go up against Josiah. He nodded and hung up the phone and headed home to get some much needed rest. He had been up for the past three days never sleeping just bossing up in Jamaica. Now that he was back him and his boys were ruthless and he wanted to live life in the lap of luxury.

Josiah lived and breathed the bay area. Whatever he wanted he got. Money was not a question; respect was not a question he got it. One day he did want a queen to reign supreme and truth be told every woman that he ran across was about themselves and money. Never loyal, never trust worthy all except for one. Paige Walton, he had a feeling of love for Paige that was deeply embedded in his DNA. He wanted her but he was waiting for the right time because she was such a good girl. As he pulled up to his condo on the strip he sat in his car for a moment.

"So what's up what do you want?"

"I miss you," she whined and he chuckled lightly while stroking his chin.

"You miss me or this dick?" he asked boisterous.

"Both to be honest nigga."

"Well see that's the problem we don't miss you," he laughed and she began to curse him out. He heard her ratchet momma and sister in the background and shook his head. He laughed and hung up the phone.

"When will these hoes learn," he said shaking his head and hoping out of the car to go inside of his house.

Once inside he finally got the call he had been waiting on.

"Word?" he answered.

"Bruh that bird coming off the plane now," Malik said to him.

"Leek watch that bitch and make sure that them bird watchers don't make that hoe fly," he spoke back to him in code and his boy understood.

"Alright." He said in final.

His stomach growled but it was never for food it was for money. Whenever Josiah was in contact with dope or money he felt his stomach growl. He walked to his kitchen and heated up his food from his mom.

"Guess this will do."

• • ❧ • •

"SO HOW DO YOU FEEL?" Kita asked her taking in her long hair. She smiled, here she was at in the streets because Kita talked her into going out to grab a bite to eat before the club.

"Girl I'm good stop asking me that," she rolled her eyes as she answered the question for the hundredth time today. Kita laughed at her annoyance.

"Look I'm just trying to make sure your straight. You know how you get."

"I know but you get so damn worried about me all the damn time, give it a break," she spoke sitting down and looking at the menu. To be honest she loved how it felt being alone not worrying about anything. She dropped 1200 on her tuition this morning and it felt good to be free. No worries, no stress, just living.

"Ok then start living some damn time," she laughed and Paige shook her head. Her iPhone vibrated and she saw that she had a text from Trey.

Even though Trey loved her to pieces she never liked him like that. She was always focused on Josiah. She loved Josiah and no one could make that ache go away that she could never have him. But she did entertain people every once in a while, and since Trey was in town that's what she did.

Sup with you?

She shook her head and giggled. Kita looked over at Paige and raised her eyebrow.

Waiting on you ☺

Word?! Well shit I'm tryna see you tonight, have that monkey spanked something vicious.

Lol you a nasty nigga..but tonight's a no go my best is having a party so I guess we have to rain check.

Or nah?! You in my city I'm a get ya lil' ass for sure. He texted in final and Paige shook her head. He was always so damn adamant when it came to meeting one another.

"So what his thirsty ass say?"

"That's its on," she giggled and Kita raised her glass.

"Then its on," they giggled and ate their food.

• • ❧ • •

JOSIAH STOOD IN HIS town house as he waited on one of his side pieces to come out of the bathroom. She was taking forever and a day when she knew that she had to make a drop and his mom was having dinner at her house.

"Mannnn come out I gotta fucking go," he knocked on the door for her to hurry.

"Nigga I'm coming," she responded back to him. He shook his head and walked into his office to check and see if Trey was where he was supposed to be.

"Wassap shotta?" Trey answered his phone.

"Wassap bruh where you at?"

"At the boat." He answered looking around.

"Ok we on the way this bitch taking forever," he rubbed his goatee in frustration. Trey laughed.

"Nigga what's new? I don't know why you press so hard you know her ass take forever."

"Alright bless," he spoke hanging up. He walked into the room just as she was walking out.

"Baby you look yummy," she took in his bond cologne, Alexander McQueen jeans and crisp white shirt. He waved her off.

"You play too fuckin' much Din," he barked at her and she smirked. She walked up to him and his 6-foot frame towered over her small 5 feet stance. She grabbed his dick and swatted her away.

"Fuck off me I got business to tend to and you with the shit." He spoke angrily.

"I'm with the shit?" she asked incredulously.

She flipped her long hair behind her ear that she inherited from her Thai descent and walked up to him and pushed him. He grabbed her wrist.

"Don't start with me, your late as fuck playing with my money. Stop playing Din, this is important you feel me?" she nodded her head and accepted him as the look in his eyes wouldn't tell her other wise.

"All you give a fuck about is deals lately, what about us? You haven't fucked me in forever." She said looking in his eyes.

"Get over it, I fuck my money that bitch is always loyal, now let's fucking go," he stated in final walking out the door.

She shook her head and gathered her thoughts. She knew that they were going down a rocky road but damn she loved this man past death and he didn't see it. She painted her smile on and got ready to ride.

3
I choose you baby...

"B*ang bang, I'm calling your name, you're like a fire the world can't tame*" Janelle Monae sang *as* Paige walked into Club Cameo as it was lit up in its prime for everyone to see. Her beautiful onyx colored skin was oiled to perfection and made her look like an extra from the movie twilight when it hit her. Her and Kita made the Olympic American dream team look bad.

"Ayyyyeeee my nigggaassss," Din yelled as she ran up. Kita and her smiled as they saw their childhood friend. She had been missing in action as of late and they all chalked it up to her being serious about schooling and work.

They all conformed into a group hug leaning down a tad bit more because of Din's Asian background. After the love that they shared Din whipped her neck in disbelief at Paige.

"Whhhhaaaatttt look at you." She said as she over looked Paige. She made her custom black and gold deep v front and back look like money. She winked at Din as she tossed the bang from in front of her face. Kita made sure she had her on display like a perfectly posed doll. Even though she wasn't used to it, she loved it.

"You like?" She twirled in a circle showing off her assets.

"Like? Me love." She smiled. Looking at Kita she looked lovely in a powder pink dress that hugged every curve that she cold have. Her nice 36 D breast sat up nicely and she enjoyed the affection.

"Kita," Din said running her hair in her brand new set of curls. Kita smiled and blew her a kiss.

"You know wassap." She laughed while bending over to twerk.

"Twerk it mama," Din screamed as she broke out in a twerk stance to join her.

"Biittcchhhhh noooooo it's nigga in here." Kita laughed straightening up as she grabbed her and laughed.

Din grabbed Paige's hand and led her to the VIP section. There was a big cake in the form of a grad hat. The ladies looked at Din and smiled. She had come so far to reach the place where she was now. Graduating at the top of her class in honors and a member of a high stepping sorority, Din was the hero. She looked at them and wiped the tears that begged to come out. Kita walked over to her and kissed her cheek then proceeded to pour everyone a bottle of her favorite drink called Skittle-tini. All the ladies held their glasses up.

"You have been the best friend to me that I have always wanted in life. I am proud of you sis, just know that this will last forever and we will always be the 3 musketeers," Kita sincerely said as Paige's smiled with tears in her eyes. They both kissed her cheek and they yelled out in excitement.

As they all began to party and dance Paige was happy she decided to come out. She needed the time to be around people who truly loved her. Stopping for a minute feeling light headed, she looked at her girls.

"Yall I'm a get up and get some air." Paige said as she got up and took a walk outside.

As the cool air hit her she looked at her phone and saw that she had a missed call from Trey. She called him back, no answer. She shrugged and rolled her eyes.

She stated as she looked around in her purse for some gum. While she bent down she felt a pair of hands lift her up. She looked into the stranger's eyes and saw that it was Trey and a very handsome guy with him. Once she paid attention she saw that the stranger was Josiah. She stared into Treys eyes trying her damndest to not look into Josiah's eyes but she couldn't help it she felt an automatic attraction. Something that she tried to fight forever. She leaned into him as he out reached his hands for a hug.

"Sup ma?" he spoke into her ear as she looked over his shoulder and peeked at Josiah. She took in his swag, he rocked nothing that the normal eye could catch but to her she knew it all. She was a student studying fashion for heavens sake.

"Nothing much, how are you I just called you." She spoke to him and he smiled.

"I know I couldn't answer I was handling some business for Josiah ass," he nodded at his him.

"Wassap P?"

"Hey," she smiled a smile that at that moment he knew that the heavens sang to him telling him that he had to have this girl. She was so beautiful and up kept and all the while that she knew him, he only caught her smile once or twice.

Pretty ass, he thought to himself. If Trey didn't have a thing for her then he would most definitely would have made her his.

He didn't give a fuck if her sister wanted him or not, he wanted her.

"Look I'm a go find this girl," he spoke to Trey.

"Where is Jahari?" she asked him.

"Shit I don't know you gotta ask her. I don't keep her in my pocket." He stated and turned around.

"Bye dumb ass." She rolled her eyes.

"Stupid ass girl." He swaged off and Paige looked at Trey and smiled.

"Didn't I tell you that I would have that ass tonight?" he kissed her neck. She giggled as she loved the feeling between his arms even though they were friends he always did things like this that made their connection deeper.

"You did say that but you aint got it yet," she smirked.

"Is that right?"

"Yup," she spoke as she turned to walk off. He shook his head.

"All that ass." He smirked as he walked behind her.

Once Paige and Trey reached VIP she caught Josiah sitting down checking out his surroundings. He was so sexy with his tatts and his cool and cold demeanor. She loved that about him. He rubbed his right hand along his goatee and licked his full juicy lips.

Fuck she thought as her and Trey sat down next to him and Trey ordered some drinks.

"Man bruh where this girl at?" Josiah spoke into Trey. Trey smiled while shaking his head. He had no clue where Din was he was too busy trying to dig Paige out.

"Shit I don't know that's your girl." Trey answered as he watched Paige twirl to the beat. She was sexy as fuck and any nigga in their right mind would be a damn fool to not wife her. He never understood why she took the safe road and dressed down and bit her tongue. She never understood her full potential.

Josiah stared at Paige as well. She was sexy and she owned it. The way she twirled her hair around and created a show was all that he cared about.

"Hi baby, I heard you were looking for me." Din said walking in his space and trying to sit on his lap. He kissed her and she was in heaven. Grabbing his hand, she tried lifting him up.

"Come on girl." He said looking at Paige as she wore a confused look on her face.

"No come on babe, I want the girls to see you." She smiled.

"Nah bring dem' over here." He pulled his phone out and began to look through it. Shaking her head, she looked at Trey, he shrugged.

"Come on," she grabbed Treys hand and led him away. Josiah didn't care, as long as someone was pleasing her needy ass.

"He gets on my nerves." Din said to Trey as they walked through the club and he tried to lead her to the bathroom. Looking up at Josiah she nodded because he wasn't watching, he was talking on his phone and most likely she knew it was going to be about business.

Dipping into the stall, he picked her up and shoved his thick dick into her.

"UMmmmmm, this some good ass pussy." Trey moaned out while closing his eyes.

"This the best dick ever." She moaned out and knew she was going to have to stop fucking him but she couldn't. Din and Trey became really close over the years that she had been around Josiah. Him going back and forth between her and Jahari was a headache she cried on a daily about their situation, then one day her and Trey had sex and there had been no more looking back.

The two fucked, and loved each other whenever they could and they saw no issue with betraying Josiah even though they knew that mistrust and dishonor was not in the cards.

"You love me?" he asked and she nodded.

"No tell me that you fucking love me." He repeated as he kissed her neck never knowing that he was leaving a passion mark.

"I love you." She moaned out.

"You leaving him?"

"All the way alone." She screamed cumming and he came inside of her. Putting her down and going to the sink to make sure she was fine she asked her friends to come to the bathroom in a text.

"My girls are coming so you have to hide. And what I tell you about nutting in me?" she asked as she placed her hand on her hip. Their love making was usually careful and precise but as of late he had become to sloppy. Cumming in her, screaming and leaving marks. She had makeup but one day she had a feeling she was going to get caught.

"Shut the fuck up." He told her as he walked up and she saw their reflection in the mirror. She smiled and shivered just from looking back at him.

As Kita and Paige walked into the bathroom Din was fixing her makeup making sure she looked flawless.

"Bitch when did you start fucking with my sister's man?" Paige asked pissed that she was in the middle of this bullshit.

"One let's be clear. That nigga don't belong to no one but him, she don't own him."

"You are dumber than I thought. Look I don't even care but I can't do this with you." Paige said walking out leaving Kita shaking her head at her.

"You foul Din, you and Trey. I know he's in here I saw him stupid ass following you. You better pray that nigga don't kill him." She whipped her hair behind her shoulder as Din's heart dropped to her feet. She was right that was way to obvious. She had to clean up her act and she needed to do it before she was dead.

• • ❧ • •

WALKING OUT THE BATHROOM she saw Josiah standing by the exit waiting for her to come out. She grabbed a shot and threw it back. She wanted to ease her mind of all the bullshit that she had been through. Ease the thoughts of her mom and dad leaving her and the thoughts of never finding her brother.

"You ok?" he asked her walking behind her and scaring her. She chuckled and nodded as the effects of her champagne and vodka shot crept up.

"I'm good Josiah, leave me alone." She turned away from him but he grabbed her arm gently but with force. Leaning his tall frame to her level and then his lips brushed her ear, he spoke deeply.

"Why you always so fucking mean to me what the fuck did I do?" he asked her staring in her eyes. Shaking her head, she tried to get him to loosen up but to no avail he wasn't budging.

"I just, you remind me of her." She blurted out.

He released her and took a step back. There was a pregnant pause between the two before he thought about something and then looked into her eyes once more.

"Can you take a ride with me?" he asked and she stared at him. The look he wore she didn't know if she should follow, but her heart tugged at her to go. So she had to follow the instructions.

"Yea."

He grabbed her hand and she felt the softness coming from his. Looking behind her she saw Kita walking out the bathroom. She saw her and smiled and gave her a thumbs up. She mouth "get ya ma." And winked.

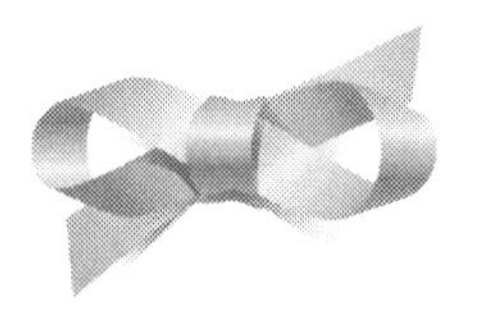

4

All I want is to love and to be loved.

Pulling into the top of the city into a place they called lovers rock, she was over looking the entire city. The view was breathtaking. She saw all the little lights making the city look as though it wasn't thousands of people living there. Hearing the engine stop she looked over at Josiah and he stared into her eyes. She felt the thumping of her heart sing to her. She was so nervous.

"Wassap?" he asked as he moved a strand of hair out of her face. She looked away as she heard Nicki Minaj sing about the crying game.

"So wassap?" he moved his hands down her face finally getting to look at her and only her.

"Nothing why did you bring me up here?"

"What you mean?"

"I mean why am I here? With you? You tryna kill me?" she asked so honestly and he laughed.

"Baby girl if I wanted to kill you I would just kill you. Not just sit her and stare at you." He laughed and she smiled.

"So a nigga gets a smile right now." He chuckled and she flipped him off.

"Oooohhhhh good girl has a bad side?" he taunted her even more.

"No I'm a good girl nigga." She giggled as he pulled his weed out and began to break it down.

She watched him roll it up and wanted to kiss him, wanted to be by his side the entire way. Catching her give him the goo goo eyes, she smiled at him once he began to stare back.

"So why are you always so mean to a nigga?" he pulled his lighter out and sparked up. He rolled his window down so that smoke wouldn't blow in her face. She looked away.

"You have Jahari, and yall always being mean and rude. Like I've always wondered what I did to you guys that yall treat me the way that yall do." She spoke sincerely with tears rolling down her eyes. Seeing the tears fall from her eyes made him feel bad as fuck. Not understanding why she was so upset he leaned into her.

"Wait chill Paige. A nigga haven't been mean to you." He pulled her over to him but she was jerking back. She was so upset that he was seeing her so vulnerable. Her words tugged at his heart as he tried to understand why she was feeling the way that she was.

Yes, Jahari was a mean bitch but Josiah cared for Paige in ways that she could never imagine. He was determined to change the way that she viewed him. All he wanted was for her to be his friend and then maybe they would blossom into something more but right now, he wanted to take his time and slow down.

He finally had her buried into his shirt and even though her mascara and makeup was making his shirt dirty he didn't give a fuck as he rubbed her back and ran his finger though her hair. She was full blood black and she had the most beautiful luxurious hair that he could think of. He loved a black woman that owned her own qualities over materialistic ones, even though he didn't mind it. He still appreciated it.

"It's ok P." he said soothingly and she nodded as her tears became none existent and she was wrapped into the scent of him again. His clothes smelled fresh. Not like clothing store fresh but fresh detergent and cologne.

Looking up into his grey eyes she felt a chill go through her body.

"Aye?" he asked lowly almost growl like.

"Yes?"

"Can I have a kiss?"

As soon as the words left his mouth and she nodded his dick grew in anticipation. He had been wanting to kiss her for over 10 years. He'd watch her prance around with Kita and Din and she was always the posed one. Books first never boys, the way her family took care of her, the love radiated off of her and he wanted so badly to have that in his life. Something positive, something loving, something that was her.

Pushing her hair back he could feel her breath slowing down. He inched towards her while grabbing her chin and placing his juicy lips onto hers. She closed her eyes and let go. He was gentle yet rough. His lip invaded her mouth as he began to tongue her down. Pulling her onto him she sat on his lap and grinded onto him. Running her fingers across his head she released a moan.

"Paige?" he asked as his dick poked her.

"Yes baby," the way she said it panged his heart. What the fuck was she doing to him, and so quickly.

"Can I taste that pussy ma?" he licked his lips as she squirmed in his seat. He placed his hands on her ass and breathed heavily.

"How?" she asked with a devilish grin. Something that she didn't know that she had in her. It was like he was bringing out her bad side and he loved it. He licked his lips and smiled.

"With my lips, then I'm a put this dick in you."

• • ❧ • •

"WHERE YO' NIGGA AT?" Jazmine asked her little sister as they sat up and club Cameo looking for him. They saw Kita and Din sitting with Trey, Malik, and Drizz. Looking around the club for her man she didn't know which way to go. Where he was or how she was going to deal with him if she caught him with another bitch.

"I came all this way for nothing?" she asked looking around and then walking towards the table where she saw everyone caked off.

"Where my nigga?" Jahari popped her gum and Din laughed and shook her head.

"Racthett ass bitch."

"Look you lil rice cake eating ass muthafucka don't start with me, where is my nigga at?" she asked as she and Jazmine stood there with mean mugs on their faces. Each lady had a sort of cute thing going for the in a weird skiddish type of way. Jazmine was the oldest but she had her nose in Jahari's business whenever need be.

"Bitch I don't know where he at now, but he just got done eating my pussy so hell who knows." Din looked at her nails unbothered as she just served tea to Jahari and it was piping hot.

Kita's mouth dropped and she knew she was going to have to beat someone's ass over her best friend. She knew how Jazmine got down and even though Jahari had been quiet for a little while she knew she was her twin, they were messy and that's what they loved to do.

"Wait what?" Jahari said as her light skin began to turn beet red. Jazmine stood there wrapping her hair into a bun.

"Yall bitches not bout to jump my bitch tho', got me fucked up." Kita said coming to them as Leek grabbed her arm back.

"Chill out ma," he grabbed her and she shook her head.

"You know what Din, I'm a wait for you." She said looking at Kita. Kita was known for throwing hands and all hoes could do was catch them. Her dad was a trained boxer so all he did was train her on how to beat someone's ass.

"Scary hoe." Kita rolled her eyes and then looked at Din. Din smirked and she shook her head and walked off. Leek went after her to calm her down.

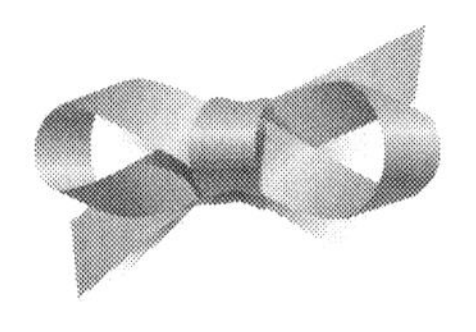

5
I'd rather be ya' nigga

Guilt, shame, and pain were the only feelings that Paige was feeling as she and Josiah finish their love making session. Not only did he fuck her mind for years, now he had her body, he fucked her soul. She had always imagined a night with him but she didn't want it like this, he belonged to her sister and she knew this would call beef that she didn't need at the moment.

"You ok?" he kissed her neck and sent chills down her spine once more. Was she ok? Hell she couldn't even answer that, all she knew was that she fucked up and she didn't know how to repair that.

"Baby?"

Her head jerked back at the sudden call of names. Baby? They graduated to pet names? Shaking her head and pulling her dress down all she wanted to do was bring relief to her aching coochie. He was well endowed and she was happy for that.

"I'm not your baby Josiah come on. We all know you got what you wanted. Fuck with the broken girl that had nothing to lower her even more. She shook her head and looked out the window.

Pulling on her chin so that she could focus on him, he smiled at her.

"You know what?"

"What?"

"I'm a be yours all yours and your gonna be all mines, and there is nothing that yo' ass can do about it, now cut that shit out." He smirked and leaned in to give her a kiss. She turned her face.

"Don't fucking play with me Pretty." She loved how he called her pussy or P. That was his own nickname for her and it excited her.

"We both know you have Jaha—"

"If I wanted her, I would be with her. I'm exactly where I wanna be." He stressed as he so intensely into her eyes and she felt her heart being torn into two. Those grey eyes were spell binding. She didn't want to get hurt but this is what she had been waiting on. Love at it finest, and did she call it love? Yes. He was her 1 in a sea of millions and she knew that since the 5th grade.

So instead of thinking, saying something smart, or even fighting she chilled and sat back as he made the engine purr and took her to his house.

• • ❧ • •

THE NEXT MORNING THE light shined brightly into her eyes and she tried to shield herself from going blind, but when she looked to the right of her she saw the most glorious tatted up brown skin body that she could have laid eyes on. His tatts were so perfectly drawn to perfection, his muscles were beefy and his skin was so smooth. She just wanted to kiss on him all day and that's exactly what she did. She began to kiss on his body as he stirred. Once he woke he looked down to see her kissing his tatts and tracing them with her fingers.

Smirking and admiring her beautiful skin he palmed her ass to let her know he was up.

"Good morning baby." He smiled and she returned the favor.

"You slept well?"

"Yeah I did, this bed is comfy as fuck." She nodded coming up and laying next to him.

Looking at his handsome features he reached over to his nightstand and grabbed his zip lock bagged filled with kush. She rolled her eyes.

"Why you got an attitude? You don't like my weed?" he asked as she eyes his tatts once more. She shook her head as she heard her phone vibrating.

Getting up and walking to get her phone he looked at her body and saw that she had a trail of butterflies from her navel spiraling down to her thigh. He licked his lips and picked up his phone. She bent over and then she heard his voice.

"When you wake up to a bad one snap... nah I don't mean just a bad bitch cuz she sexy as fuck."

She shrieked and ran over to him grabbing him.

"Aye don't knock my fucking weed out my hand tryna' grab my damn phone bruh." He smacked her ass hard and she winced in pain.

"Betta pipe yo' ass down." He said snatching his phone and she began to pout. She didn't want to be on his snap, his insta, not a damn site. They were already doing too much by moving the way they were moving. She felt so foul for this.

He pulled his phone out again at the same time as he lit his blunt while laying on top of her.

"Get yo; fat ass off of me." she whined until he pushed his dick deep into her. She moaned out in ecstasy. Taking a hit of the weed and blowing it into her mouth she closed her eyes and felt euphoric. He pulled began recording on his phone and she tried to hide her face.

"Baby?" he spoke voice shaken with lust as he plunged back into her.

"Hmmmmm." She closed her eyes enjoying every moment.

"Look at the fucking camera baby." He bit her lip and snapped the picture.

"Stop being so fucking shy with me. I've been knowing you..."

"Mmmmhhmmmm," she moaned out as he hit her spot. He could feel her tremble.

"Fuck this pussy too good." He couldn't finish his blunt or his sentences as he slipped into her wetness. He knew he fucked up by not wrapping up and he prayed that she wasn't dirty. But the more he thought about who he was with, and how good she felt he was on the verge of tapping out.

"Fuckkkk," she moaned out as she came on him and not being able to hold it he released inside of her.

"Fuck." He turned and laid on his back, while relighting the blunt.

"You came in me Josiah."

"I know baby." He kissed her forehead before she got up to go clean up.

• • ❧ • •

JANNIKA AND JAHARI stood in the backyard as Jazmine and Jessica cleaned up the backyard. They were seeing where they would set up the balloons, plates and more. They were having a just because bar-b-Que in a day and couldn't wait to see how everything would turn out.

"Mama, this looks good." Jazmine said walking over to her mom and digging into her potato salad without washing her hands. Smacking her hands and ready to go in, Jazmine laughed and ran out the way. Looking over at Jahari who was looking for her man since last night, she shook her head.

Jazmine was once there and she knew that she was stressed.

"Where the fuck is this nigga at? I'm worried, I think something happened to him." She turned to Jazmine and shook her head.

"It's been too damn long for him not to call me."

She began to think about what Din said last night. Was she really fucking her nigga?

"Girl." Jessica hummed. Shaking her head at her sister's stupid antics she didn't even have anything to say. She was always the one they never listened to so she rarely interacted with them. She loved Paige. They grew so close sharing a room they learned so much about one another.

Even though they were both far apart in age, she didn't get alone with Jaz or Jahari. She hated them and hated how they treated her.

Pulling her phone out she texted Paige and asked her when she would be home. She figured she just spent the night at Kita's house. So she didn't think anything of her and Josiah.

"Who is this bitch?" Jahari spat as she looked at her phone while looking at Josiah snapchat. She saw the girls body and tattoo and she had to admit the bitch was bad but her long ass hair was covering her face.

"When I find out who the fuck this bitch is, I'm a beat her face in."

"That's what your ass gets." Jessica smirked and walked off. Leaving her sister and mom to talk shit.

• • ❧ • •

"AYE BABE?" JOSIAH STOOD in the shower as Paige stood staring at the hickies on her neck. She was shocked that she had so many, hell she was shocked that she was acting the way she was acting, knowing damn well this boy was with her sister.

"Yes Siah?" she said coming into the bathroom in her boy shorts, one of his tees and tall tube socks. He licked his lips and thought about getting in her pussy again. He had never been the type to be so sprung off pussy but he wanted more just by staring at her sexy ass.

"Baby can you come in here and wash my back." He smiled and her heart fluttered. She stared into his eyes, as hers traveled down to his ripped six pack, his brown skin made her lick her lips and the way that the water cascaded on him made him look better than any lame ass model she saw in a book. She wanted to kiss on his tatts and have him pull her hair as they fucked wildly in the shower.

"Baby?" he smirked as he caught her staring at the monster that brought her weak to the knees.

"Huh?"

"Bring that ass in here." He tried to grab her but she backed up.

"No Siah I have to much stuff to do today, plus they are having a party tomorrow and I need to go set up. Are you coming tomorrow?"

He was silent.

"Ok, well Kita is on her way to pick me up."

Raising his eyebrow and stared at her.

"What?"

"Why the fuck you leaving me? and I don't give a damn about what they got going on over there, shit why do you? They treat you so fucked up but on God daddy gone handle that shit baby." He nodded to himself as if confirming with her. S

he shook her head and walked out the bathroom. He obviously didn't need his back washed anymore and she had to get dressed before Kita got there.

• • ❧ • •

"LEEK STOOPPPPP," KITA giggled as she rolled out of bed. She and Malik had been recovering from a long night of pleasure and they both didn't want to let the other go.

"Hell nah, fuck with a nigga today man, I gotta go take care of some business but aint you going to the bar-b-Que?"

He asked as she looked into his pretty browns. She was blessed to have been with him. They had been messing around for a couple years but last night she was tired of coming home to an empty bed, so after the club let out and she wanted someone to hold her and care. He was right there for her and she appreciated that about him.

"No Leek I gotta go pick up Paige." She wrapped her finger around one of his long skinny dreads.

"What?" he asked pulling her closer so she could feel him.

"Paige nigga, she's at Siah house." He nodded his head as he watched her get up and handle herself before walking out the door.

Once Kita was out the door she felt relieved as she always did. She was going crazy because he did things to her that no one else could do. She hated the fact that she would always run back to him. Driving over an hour to pick up her friend she eased into the nice neighborhood of row houses and loved where he was living. It looked so peaceful and calm. Taking out her cell phone she called Paige.

"Hey bestie I'm outside." Kita said as she pulled up to Josiahs door.

"Ok I'm on my way out."

Kita sat in the car and waited for Paige to come out but thought about Leek and his last words.

• • ❧ • •

"SO YOU COMING BACK tonight?" Josiah asked as he threw his shorts on.

"Coming back for what Siah?" she asked as she grabbed her shoes.

"Come on now so you gone play with a nigga?" looking deeply into her eyes he was trying to see if she placed voodoo on him.

Sighing and thinking about it. She was going to just do it, she was tired of playing games with love. She was tired of never having her way.

"Yea," she sighed.

"Well I'm a come pick you up." He kissed her lips and swagged off to the kitchen shaking her head and walking out the door she knew it was going to be some bullshit today.

Walking over to the car Kita looked up and then looked back again. Seeing her best friend in a shirt and boxers she smiled and gave her the thumbs up.

"Sooooo I'm guessing that dick was good bitch." She laughed.

Paige squeezed her legs closed just thinking about Josiah again. He was worth it all. She knew that it would take work, she didn't trust him, and she knew she was going to have to fight but she was ready.

"Was it?!" she saw Kita spark up a blunt. She knew that only meant one thing she was happy. Kita only smoked when she felt the need too. She mostly did this when she was happy and nothing else.

"Girl me and Leek decided to make shit official."

Raising her eyebrow at her, she forgot how much of a cat and mouse game they played with one another. They had so much love for one another but yet they were so different that it hurt. Nodding her head and smiling she was happy they were finally in their happily ever after's. Hers was more flawed then happy but that was fine, she was ready for that. She was ready to play the role of being the hood wife.

As she neared her house she dreaded having to do the walk of shame. She didn't want anyone in her business. Looking at Kita who was in her own world. She didn't want to have one but she she had to support her family. Pulling up to the house, she was ready to get out and go on about her business.

"Ok, well shit I guess ill see you later." She smiled and she nodded.

"See you later bae." She kissed her cheek and went in the house.

Walking into the house, she smelled the good cooking of Jannika and couldn't wait to get something to eat. She loved soul food and even though some days they would eat all the food and leave her with scraps Jessica always looked out for her.

"Where your fast ass been?" Jazmine asked as she stared her down. Placing her hand up and waving her off she went to her room.

"And you better be down her in 30 minutes to clean up." Jannika yelled.

"Yes step-mother" she responded under her breath.

5

No games I'm done...

W*YD?*

Paige smiled as her phone vibrated in class. It was Friday and she had a night class and was so tired from fucking round all day. Listening to her professor lecture was not in her plans tonight.

In Class... can I live?

She smiled as she placed her phone back down and shook her head.

Fuck nah... let me pick you up I miss you nigga

She smiled and shook her head as she looked around and her eyes landed on a boy in class he was smiling at her and she returned the favor. She was about to text him back until she started hearing everyone get out of their seat and move around. She looked and her friend nodded at her. She got up and sat by him, "Thank you." She told him as she focused on their group work and would have to wait to cake.

• • ❧ • •

2 CHAINZ STARTED TO sing out as Josiah sat in front of his red Audi A8 in his hood as him Leek, and Drizz talked shit with the niggas on the block.

"Aye bruh when these niggas be singing and shit they be gay as fuck my nigga." Leek laughed and Drizz shook his head.

"Nigga you be listening to this shit tho'" he laughed and she Leek waved him off.

"Bruh this Van shit." He nodded his head just thinking bout her white ass. He was low-key in love with her.

"Nigga yea right, you love these R&B niggas." Josiah laughed out and they joined in.

Just give me all of you in exchange for me

Josiah's heart sped up as he felt a cramp in his stomach. If Paige wanted him that was already a given factor. He was going to make sure she never questioned what they had.

Baby you got my soul

He texted her back as he blew down on the weed, and he meant every word that he spoke. "Aye there go your girl." Drizz pointed as he looked up and saw Jahari walking down the block. Here it was 8 at night and she was walking around with her sister being a thot. Shaking his head, he knew he had to let this go before it went further than it was supposed to.

Jahari and Jazmine were the hoods most ratchetest girls that they had known. Short skirts, shorts, dresses and this was all in the winter. The young him never tripped off of her antics but where he saw himself going he wanted no parts in her.

"Ayyeeee baby." Jahari said as she walked over showing her ass. Shaking his head, he slid his hands into his pockets and she licked her lips. She couldn't help it; she knew she lucked up with him. Paid, on top of his business, and he never let her go hungry. She loved him. Wrapping her small arms around him she sensed he was colder today than most. She wondered why but she didn't ask, for the fear of him telling her words that might hurt.

Taking her hands off of him he looked at Jahari and tried to see if he was making a mistake, but no matter what he kept seeing nothing in her that he wanted to obtain. She was ran through and had no life, just a shell.

"What's wrong?" she asked looking around.

"Lets go talk," he led her to his car as he left his friends behind. Her sister looked at her to make sure she was ok, but she didn't make any eye contact.

*Please don't let him break my heart lord...*she prayed.

Once in his car, he scratched his head and turned to her. His gold Rolex was glistening in the car light.

"You look nic—"

"Look this shit, I can't do it no more." He told her straight out.

"What?" she asked as her fear came to truths. He was leaving her and she didn't know why.

"I need to leave this shit we got going alone. You need someone that's on your level, as I need someone on mines." He told her and then waited. She took a deep breath and stared at him in the face.

"What? The. Fuc—-" she started but then caught herself. She didn't want to come off rude, or brash, not this time. She wanted to be right for him.

"You really leaving me? why baby?"

"I need to do other things."

"It's a bitch?" she asked with tears in her eyes. She knew he had found someone else. She knew it, she could feel it in her body.

"Baby look, just do you and I'll still be here for you. I'm a always—-" holding his hand up to cut her off, she knew that he meant business and he wasn't going to be with her. Shaking her head, she began to cry but not before she allowed him to feel how she felt.

"You leaving me?" she asked and she shook his head in disbelief of how bad she was taking it.

"Nigga, nah you aint fucking leaving me." she cried as she cocked her hand back and slammed fire to him. Then delivered a blow to his face. Trying to grab her hands she started wailing on him and kicked his dashboard.

"Bitch you crazy?" he yelled out as Drizzy, Leek and Jazmine rushed to the doors.

"Yup, I'm crazy, you think you can leave? Nigga you aint leaving me," she scratched his face up and when she saw blood she laughed. Opening the door and grabbing her Jazmine pulled her away.

"I swear, get your sister for a I fucking kill her."

Pointing at Jazmine so she would understand that he was going to hurt her, he was ready for her to get out of his sight.

"I hate you." She screamed as her sister was carrying her to their car. Shaking his head and looking at her face he was pissed.

Hoping in his car he sped off to his house to take care of hisself and then to handle some business.

• • ❧ • •

"YOU KNOW WHAT'S CRAZY? Paige asked her classmate as they walked down the corridor. He was so lost in her pretty eyes. She was flawless effortlessly as she walked down the hall with her hair up into a bun, sweat pants, and a sweat shirt. It was so cold and windy so she didn't try to dress up or impress anyone.

"What?" he smiled as they walked towards the parking lot. She was going to ride with him as she did every Friday.

"The way that Professor Ad—" she was cut short by a honking and someone stepping out of their cherry red car. She looked and noticed that it was Josiah. Looking towards him, she smiled.

"You know him?" Her classmate David asked. She nodded.

"Yea, I'll be ok, Thanks for the ride though." She smiled and gave him a hug.

He smiled and kissed her cheek and climbed into his car as she pranced over to Josiah. Once she walked up to him, she saw that he was matching her in sweats and Lebrons. She smiled at him and leaned over to give him a hug.

"Nah get in the car."

Feeling some type of way about how he turned her down, she rolled her eyes and climbed into the seat as he closed the door and walked over to his side. Looking at him in confusion she could tell he wasn't there with her. After 30 minutes of silence and driving from the college to his house, she broke the ice as they were crossing the bridge.

"Where are you?"

"What?" he asked glancing at her.

"Your somewhere else." Pointing to his head she tried to figure out why he was just staring at the road.

"Who the fuck was that you were hugging?"

Jerking her head to stare at him, she wondered was he tripping off of this the entire time. Shaking her head, she giggled.

"You serious?"

"Quit fucking playing with me."

"That's just Davi—"

"If I ever catch another nigga hands on you, or you on another nigga, on life I'm a kill him. And send his momma the parts he touched you with."

He was so cold and callous that she knew he wasn't joking. Nodding her head and looking out the window she felt a sense of belonging in a weird way. Smiling she unbuckled her seat belt and slinked over to him.

"What you doing?"

She slid partially into his lap and kissed his lips.

"I don't feel like waiting." She whispered in his ear as she felt his dick spring to life. Then she paid attention to his face and saw the marks on his face.

"What the fuck is this?" she asked as she slid back into the seat. She was no longer feeling the exchange any longer. She was turned off. She knew that she saw Jahari, she did this to him on a regular whenever they would fight she would mark him up.

"What you mean?" he kept driving while getting off at their stop.

"What the hell do you mean?" she looked at him.

"I told Hari we couldn't be together any longer.

It was silence in the car as they pulled up to his house. She sat in the car with her arms folded. She didn't want to get out the car and see his face, why? All she could think about was what she did to him, or if they had sex together, or if what he was saying was bullshit.

"Take me the hell home."

She pouted as soon as he opened the door to get her out.

"You aint going no where, but in here so I can sleep man."

"Did you fuck her tonight?"

Arms folded she looked like a brat for the first time and that made him horny as fuck. Walking to the door to unlock it, he looked back at her and then went into the house. Wiping her eyes as she wanted to cry for not trusting in this relationship, not knowing what she wanted to do, not knowing if she really wanted this her heart was tugging to go home and stay single.

Her feet moved into the house, she was afraid of what might happen she just didn't want to get played. As soon as she opened the door Siah was standing there waiting for her. He grabbed her hand and hugged her.

"I need you." He kissed her forehead and led her up the steps to the bedroom.

• • ❧ • •

SATURDAY JAHARI, JAZMINE and Jannika were greeting people as guest began to pour in. They were ready for the festivities to begin. Jazmine turned up the sound system as everyone grabbed their drinks, food, and got the weed going. Jahari was sitting in a corner not sure of what was going on. She knew she had fucked up when she scratched his face up, but she wasn't sure if it was over.

"What's wrong baby?" Jannika asked as she stood by her daughter with a stack of mail. Handing her her portion she opened one that had Paige's name on it. Opening it, she saw that it was her monthly letter and a check, It was signed by her brother Daryl for 10,000. She quickly tucked the letter into her bood. Peeping her moms demeanor but shaking it off Jahari looked over at her and shook her head.

"Nothing much ma." She smiled.

"It's that nigga huh? Girl you better suck that nigga dick and go on about life. It's way too many lil' niggas with stacks. Better boss up." Grabbing her beer she tooted it up and walked off.

Jannika never understood why her daughters were so dumb when it came to men. She knew that in life she had to use people. Everyone plays the fool and with her it was always.

As the day went on, Kita, Paige, Drizz, Leek, and Siah were all at the turn up. Everyone was mellow and chill enjoying one another's company. Josiah was pissed that Paige had been ignoring him all day. After their night together he thought shit was cool, but he thought wrong. As soon as she walked into the house she was cold once more and they were at square one.

Getting upset as he saw her in dudes faces, he followed her to the kitchen as she walked to get more drinks. Going into the fridge, she was so hungry but she didn't want to eat. She had been trying to reprogram Josiah out of her mind all day, but was having such a hard time doing so.

Backing up and feeling someone on her ass, she looked back into his grey eyes and bit her lip.

"So you acting hella funny?"

Rolling her eyes she came up and looked at him. Walking over to the counter, she placed the drinks there and leaned back.

"I don't feel like doing this shit any more Josiah, what more can we do? You belong to her."

"Man shut the fuck up."

She pushed him back as he walked on her.

“No, I can’t Josiah I just cant do this anymore. Your thinking about you and never about me.”

His eyes looked into her soul as he felt as though he was defeated. He was scared that she was serious this time. He didn’t know what else to do to prove to her that he was about them.

"That shit hurts a nigga to his core that you think like this about me ma," Josiah spoke with fear laced thick in his voice. The last person that he wanted to lose was Paige. She had been his oxygen for years and even though they weren’t together she still kept him going with her spirit. Now that she was shutting him out, he didn't know how to open the door she was closing.

Turning around he got a glimpse of her juicy derrière that he loved to rub on. She walked to the cabinets to grab more things for the party, walking over to her slowly she felt like she was being stalked and he most definitely was the stalker. Her breath became shallow and erratic. Easing behind her and placing his hands on the counter so that she had nowhere to run he leaned down and her scent aroused him.

"Fuck, Paige don’t do this shit to me." His manhood grew in length, begging to be freed just to please her. He never wanted to be with her sister but Paige was always so timid and so humbled that he couldn't imagine breaking her. He always wanted her to be his prized possession. Jahari was always so straight forward and ratchet. She knew what she wanted and even though they started off as fuck friends they grew into a mutual relationship.

Looking down at his tatted arms she felt weak, she was determined not to give in like the time before this. She needed to be set free from the hell hole she was in. She saw how her best friend became a side chick and she glorified it, that wasn't Paige and she wasn't going to allow it to happen. Kissing her neck and making her heartbeat slow with the time Paige began to come to reality. She couldn't do it, not unless he was hers fully and by the looks of things Josiah Foster would never be hers. It hurt like hell but she was a strong woman and she would be sure keep it that way. Turning around to tell him to stop he lifted her on the counter and sat her in a position that her ass fit perfectly in his palms.

"Josiah I have loved you since I was in the 5th grade, you have been my best friend, but what we are doing can never happen again." She looked into his deep hazel stone gray eyes and wrapped her arms around him for the last time as they shared one last hug. She wished she could leave him but she couldn't stare into his eyes. She sat right on the counter and kissed him openly.

"Yea that's right baby, tell a nigga what you want." He bit her lip and she laughed. She wasn't giving up for no one. Opening her up some more and dipping his fingers deep into her canal she moaned out loud. She didn't give a damn who was around, she didn't care who was watching. She just wanted to live, she just wanted to be free. She just wanted him.

"You little fucking bitch." They heard a voice creep behind them. Biting her lip and closing her eyes she knew that this would happen. She knew that the bullshit would follow but she didn't care and neither did he. Once he had her sweetness last night he made up his mind that there was no going back.

Pulling up his pants and turning around, he looked behind him and saw Jahari standing there with tears rolling down her face. She looked heart broken. Placing his hands over his face he turned to look at Paige.

"You ok?"

Feeling the sting from his questioning, she reached around and smacked Paige.

"Yea bitch, you o—" Before she could finish her statement she was followed with a quick push and then a set of hands were over her. She looked to see who it was and it was Paige.

"I'm so tired of you," she said with tears falling from her eyes. She was releasing the last years that she was in that house, beaten, abused, and did wrong. She never once did her wrong, she never once made her feel as if she wasn't at home. Did she feel bad about what she was doing? Yes she did, but she didn't mean to do the things that's she did.

"I hate you." She screamed as people piled into the house, no longer caring about the kids who were outside putting on a show for the adults. Paige was beating the hell out of Jahari.

"No, you little bitch." Jannika said as she saw Paige on top of her daughter getting the best of her.

"Jazzzz!" she yelled out knowing that Jessica was no help.

Walking over to get some hits in on Paige she was stopped by Kita and an on looking Josiah. He had no issues hitting on a woman if need be especially over his.

"Baby, Baby." He pulled Paige up when he felt like Jahari got her ass beat enough. Huffing and puffing she looked around at everyone gawking at her as if she was a monster.

"What?" she asked outloud upset.

"Bitch get out of my house." Jannika spoke as Jazmine rushed in to get her sister but cutting her eyes at her.

"Your house?"

Paige looked on incredisiously.

"Your house?" she walked towards her and she felt a bit of fear in her heart.

"You think my daddy made this house for you?" she looked around at how the beautifully kept house was tattered and torn. It matched the mood of the people staying in it.

"My daddy built this house for his family, his wife, his two children. He worked hard with his bare hands for us. This isn't your house."

Looking at her and daring her to say a word Paige walked to the counter and grabbed her bag.

"Bitch I will die before I let you take it." Jannika smirked as Paige slowly walked to her. She got close enough so that only she could hear and spoke slow and precise so that she couldn't get anything mixed up.

"That wouldn't be a problem." She said in final before looking at her daughters. She smiled at Jessica and then turned to walk off. Her, Josiah, Kita, Leek, and Drizz walked out and left them to wallow in hurt.

As the year went by...

As spring turned to summer and summer to fall the seasons changed and the love that Paige and Josiah shared grew strong and magnificent. They were learning so much about one another for the first year, that now they were finally enjoying the love that they shared. It was now two years after the altercation of her and Jahari and it was Paiges favorite season, Winter.

The nippy air, and joyful sounds of family and fun was most definitely in the air, but she couldn't focus on anything and even though she was doing all that she could do to stay happy and away from her estranged family. But things were hard at the moment, she was fighting for her family's house and it was the hardest things that she could have been dealing with. Josiah had gotten her a lawyer but she wanted more support, she wished her brother was around.

Sitting up in her all white Honda as she ordered some of the best curly fries with chili on them in the entire city; she was thinking about a way to go about it. She hated that she wouldn't give her back her mommas and daddys house. Shaking her head, she looked down at her phone and smiled. It was her man.

Josiah and Paige had been together for a year, and she was loving it. She loved the attn., she loved that he gave her love on the regular but she also loved the fact that he was a man. He reminded her of her dad. A thug with a little bit of street in 'em.

"Hi babe." She answered cheerfully. Since she had been with him, she never had a worry. He made sure that she was well taken care of, she had it all and that was vocal. He at times hated that she was too vocal. He turned his sweet little Paige into a G.

"Shit what you doing?"

"In san Leandro getting some fries. Why? Where you at?"

"Shit riding through the town just left Leek and Driz ass, about to get ready to come home. Bring a nigga some food."

"Nigga food? You need some food?"

"Yea a nigga need some food baby." He smiled on the other end as they played with one another. Thinking back to how sweet, quiet and humbled she was years ago when they got together she was nothing like the woman she was today. She was a thick little fire cracker and she always spoke her mind no matter what. He fucked her into talking to him so many times that now she didn't bite her tongue and if she did it was because she wanted to play that role and get the dick heavy.

"Yea and some pussy." He spoke deeply into the phone and she closed her legs tightly as she felt the cum dripping from her legs. He had that effect on her and she knew that she was warped. Shaking her head she smirked.

"Whatever."

"Yea that's what the fuck I thought big shot." He laughed and she joined in.

"So wassap? What you tryna do?"

She opened the door after getting herself together and allowed for her black pumps to hit the ground and the wind to whip through her hair. Looking around she scoped out the building before going in that was another habit she picked up from him. When fucking with a street nigga, you had to be on your toes at all times.

"I'm a be at the house after this babe."

"Ok cool." She nodded as she walked in and ordered their food.

"I'll see you when I'm there."

"Ok, love you."

"I love you too."

And like that they ended their call and she sat down to get comfortable. Her perfectly painted nails, bunned up hair, pretty mocha skin. She knew she was ready to move on she just wanted her parents house.

Hearing the door open and the feeling the cold chill she didn't turn around she didn't want it to be a nigga who thought they could fuck with her.

"Paige?" the man yelled out and she hopped out so excited that she was getting called quickly.

"Thank you." She smiled as she grabbed the food and turned to walk out. Walking out someone grabbed her hand and she looked up only to find that it was her old friend Vanilla.

"Hey baby girl." Vanilla smiled and looked her up and down. She took in how she looked, how posed she was, and how kept she looked.

"Hey girl." She pulled her in for a hug and smiled. It had been over a year since she saw her and she was looking good. She had gained some weight, her hair was cut into a sleek bob and the tan made her look as though she was now light skinned. She looked great and Paige was no hater.

"Heyyyy," she squeezed her.

"So bitch I see that nigga Siah treating you well." She smiled while stepping back and taking her in.

"Huh?" Paige asked a little taken aback.

"I said Siah taking care of you. Bitch you know everybody in the hood know he got that pussy on lock. Left Jahari ass and finally got you a real one huh?" She giggled and moved her hair from her perfectly chiseled face. Paige shook her head and whipped her head around. Someone that she had actually missed was now acting like everyone else.

"Girl," she couldn't even finish off her sentence as she walked out the door and got into her Honda. She didn't feel like arguing with a basic bitch whom, she thought was her friend at a point. Even though her and Drizz dated, they would be around one another at some point and would be cool, so she didn't understand why she was acting this way.

Watching Vanilla run out behind her and knock on the window she rolled it down.

"Girl you took this the wrong way."

"Nah Van, you listen to me, you and them hoes in the hood. I put me on, not Siah, not anyone else. I'm a grown ass woman and worked hard as hell to get here." She said as she watched Vanilla open and close her mouth while zooming off down the block.

It took Paige 30 minutes to get home as she whipped through the streets and pulled up to their townhome. Hoping out and grabbing their bags she was pissed. She was so tired of people saying that he put her on, or that he made her what she was when the truth was, she did it on her on. She made sure she studied and she made sure that she stacked enough money to open her studio.

Stomping into the house the fluffy white carpet made her feel a little stress free along with the bath & body works Marshmallow Fireside scented candle that burned freely. She made sure that their house stayed clean and fresh. It had been a long road behind them and they overcame a lot. She had trust issues being that Josiah was such a pretty boy and all the hoes wanted him. At times she was happy that she was his girl, but at times she wasn't. This was one of those times.

Placing their food on the counter and grabbing hers out of the bag she pulled her fries out and began to pick her food with her fork.

"I can't fucking believe that shit." She began as she picked up her phone to call Kita, she knew either Kita was sleeping or she was fucking. She must had been doing one of the two because she didn't answer the phone. Sighing and rolling her eyes, she was tired.

She took a bite but her anger would not subside. Hearing the door open and close, she didn't look back as she knew it was Siah. She could feel his body presence, smell his cologne and as soon as she looked down his arms were wrapping around her. Biting her lip she looked at him as he kissed her chin. The connection that they shared was magical and deep. Something that she knew she could never pass up. No matter what she knew she was stuck, really stuck with or without him. She couldn't leave him.

"Wassap mama?"

He reached around and took a bite of her food while looking at his phone and placing it on silent. Whenever he was in the house he made sure that she had his undivided attention.

Pushing back and slamming her food down she rolled her eyes.

"Wassap?"

"You wont even believe who I ran into today."

She closed her eyes and placed her fingers on her temples. Looking back at her and shaking her head he just didn't understand what she was going through.

"Wassap?"

"I saw Van, she was tryna tell me that muthafuckas think that you saved me from the hood and shit. Like you a fucking savior." She spat angrily as her hands stretched over her thick thighs, and into her back jean pocket.

"You mad?" he asked her as he walked into her evading her space.

"What?" she rolled her eyes.

"You heard me."

"Yes I'm mad Siah."

"Fuck you mad for?" he asked as he walked to the bar and got a cup to pour something for him to chill on. He never understood why she was so upset when people said that.

"Cuz, im not no fairy tale ass bitch nigga." She rolled her eyes and stared at him.

"Mama come on, I need you to drive me to Saks. I wanna get you some new shit." He smirked and placed the car keys down for her. She shook her head and decided to get over it but it was in the back of her mind and she was sure to talk with him about it later.

But I'm not sure that you want me/ But I now know/ You know I know that this ain't right Cause you want me cause I got dough/ Ever since you walked in inside my foreign, slam my door You know I know that you been on it But I been on it, on the low[1]

Paige pushed the Audi as Josiah sat in the passenger side with his hand gripping her ass. Singing Torey Lanes. He had his head back as he zoned off into his instagram and snapchat. It was rare for him to be in the passenger side and whenever he did he rode the same way with his hands gripping her ass.

Looking at her they looked so raw and uncut. She was dressed in all white to match him. Versace and Chanel down. Even though they were still hood and down to earth, he was going it spend the money as he made it. Thanking God for blessing him with her, he leaned back and chilled for the first time without complaining about her choice of music.

Once they got to Saks she went through looking at things to buy him for Christmas, ordering things and making them ship to her PO box, she was excited for this years holidays. Picking up a pair of Alexander Mcqueens she smiled to herself thinking if she should buy them.

"Throw that shit on the counter." Josiah spoke in her ear as he slid his arms around her and rested his hands on her kitten. Leaning her head back and kissing his chin she moaned a lil' out of habit.

"Daddy I don't want to get them they are too expensive."

"How much they cost?" he asked as his breathing became shallow and he inched her towards the dressing room. Lately they had been getting it in all over the place. Feeling her kitten

---

1. *http://genius.com/7827820/Tory-lanez-say-it/But-im-not-sure-that-you-want-me-but-i-now-know-you-know-i-know-that-this-aint-right-cause-you-want-me-cause-i-got-dough-ever-since-you-walked-in-inside-my-foreign-slam-my-door-you-know-i-know-that-you-been-on-it-but-i-been-on-it-on-the-low*

thump in excitement she shoo her head, "I don't know." She answered him in between him assaulting her neck.

Her neck to him was his favorite place on her body along with her ass and stomach. He took extra care of those places. Placing her n the room, he was finally able to do as he pleased with her. As he unbuckled his pants he gave her a look that spoke volumes to her and made her take her clothes off.

"Take them jeans off, I need that."

She shimmed out of her pants and he picked her up. Within minutes she was sliding down his pole. The room walls were getting pounded upon with no mercy and he didn't give a damn.

"Ahhhhh, babe, please don't stop."

Yelling out in pleasure for the entire store to hear, she didn't give a damn. That was a habit that she acquired and she knew would be hard to stop doing. He made her talk to him while he was assaulting his pussy.

"Pretty talk to me, how this dick feel? Tell daddy how this dick feel."

"Ummmmm Daddy it's so damn good." She hummed as she felt the cum creep on her. He knew he wasn't going to be able to hold his nut in for some reason her pussy had been feeling juicer, wetter and she was mastering the art of her muscles.

"I'm cumming daddy."

"Fuck I'm nutting." He said as he emptied into her and she came down on him feeling more euphoric tan ever. Panting as she slid down off his thickness she bit his lip.

"You gonna make me have a baby."

"That's kinda the point right?" he smirked as he took the shoes and looked at em. 2100 read the price tag. Walking out of the dressing room the entire stores eyes were on him. Looking at the attendant she wore a look of astonishment.

"I need these in a 8."

He placed the shoe in her hand and sat back on the bench and waited for Paige.

• • ❧ • •

"THIS BITCH IS RUNNING around living my life, loving my nigga and reaping the benefits." Jahari slurred as she sat in the strip club and talked to her regular. It had been a year since she came into the high scale establishment and told herself that she wouldn't make it a living. Here it was going on her anniversary and she was still stuck in the same place as before.

Looking to the side and watching Vanilla talk to someone she shook her head. Vanilla danced on the regular but she did it behind Drizz's back. She would never let him know she was doing the things that she did. Hell he would kill her. Looking back at her customer she wondered why he was here. It had been over a year that she saw him. He looked god now too. Before he was skin and bones, now he was beefed up, dark skin healthy and he looked kept.

"So D, tell me about you?"

She rubbed his arm and he smiled at her showing her his handsome features.

"Well, what you wanna know?"

His Cartier shined under the lights as he smoothed out his jeans and looked over at his partner in crime. Xaylin Foster, he was from a crime mob family as well. He looked cool chilling and drinking.

"Well I have a question."

"Wassap?"

"I wanna make a nigga go away."

Raising his eyebrown and staring at her he wondered what this nigga could have done for her to want to do anything of that sort. She didn't see, like the crazy type. It seemed as though she was just a woman scorned. Waving her off and taking a shot he laughed.

"Yo' ass is crazy girl. I'll see you next time." He put his moto jacket on and walked towards Xaylin.

"D?" she called out and he turned around.

"Wassap?"

"Can you tell me your real name?" she was so innocent looking and hee knew she wanted saving, but he wasn't in that business. He was just saving himself from a life he fought so hard to not create.

"It's Daryl baby." He winked and she smiled as he walked off to join his crew. Taking another shot she looked over at Vanilla. She remembered that she heard her talking to Drizz about a move they had to make earlier in the dressing room. She knew it would be him, Leek and Josiah. Picking up her phone she called the tip line.

"Oakland PD, how may I help you."

"I need to speak to someone in charge of your narcotics department and fast." She smiled as she downed her drink. She was going to make sure they paid for her hurt and humiliation.

7
Look Good for Ya'

"Nigga you talking bout yo bitch, Van?" Josiah laughed as he Leek, and Drizzy sat at Leek's house talking shit and catching up.

"Hell yea nigga. Van nasty as fuck bruh, I mean I never had a bitch that's as nasty as her. She gargle that shit." Drizz laughed as he ran his hands over his face just thinking about how deep her throat game is.

"Yo' Van gone give ya' ass something." Leek picked up the blunt that Kita rolled up for him before she left.

"Nigga yea a baby. I'll kill that bitch on my mama." Leek laughed and Siah picked up his phone. He wanted to pick up Paige on time and didn't want to waste any time. They hadn't been together in a while and he wanted to show her that she was appreciated.

"Aye bruh yall talked to Trey?" Siah asked as he sipped on his Ace of Spades. His gold Balmain shoes glistened in the light as he sat and worried about his brother.

"Nah I aint heard from the nigga. He been real low key since he touched back down. I heard him and Din had been fucking 'round."

"That's crazy." He said lighting his blunt. He didn't really give a damn that he was fucking Din. She was a hoe and he ran through her, so if Trey was in love, then so be it. He was worried that Trey was being distant because of her and many other reasons and he didn't want that.

"Bruh wait a minute though. Why that bitch Jahari came through to the club looking for you?" Drizzy said hitting Josiahs leg. Raising his brow and shaking his head he thought about her for a second.

"For what?"

"Asking if you and Paige still together, saying how she wish she had another chance. I damn there had to stop Kita silly pregnant ass from beating her ass." Leek said in final as he fired up the PS4.

"That bitch is off I swear. A nigga never would have fucked her if I knew she was going to be that crazy."

"Shit, nigga everybody was telling you she was scandalous as fuck."

Shaking his head, he knew what Leek said was true. He never listened though, he blamed it on the fact that she was young and stupid. He most definitely knew that he was doing better, he hadn't called, texted, or saw her in 2 years. He was fully committed to Paige and he was going to stay that way.

Hearing the door open and seeing Kita walk in with her phone to her ear she smiled at them and placed her bags on the floor. Cherry red hair, ample ass, she was wearing her pregnancy well and everyone knew it. She was now 4 months pregnant and she was happy that she was able to give her man a baby after numerous tries.

"Hi brother." She said hugging Josiah and Leek.

"Don't be hugging these hoe ass nigga baby." Leek said running his hands across her stomach.

"You fed my baby?"

She nodded her head as she was about to sit on his lap but change her mind. Getting up and walking away she looked back at him and winked.

"Aye sis?"

"Wassap?"

She stopped looking back at Siah. She knew he wanted to know if Paige was done with her art gallery.

"She done?"

"Yea." She winked and walked up the steps.

"You got that shit I told you?" he asked and she nodded.

"Good looking." He yelled out while he got up.

"You owe me."

"I got you." He told her meaning every word.

"Aye, we leaving tonight?" he asked them.

They head been trying to meet up with a woman in Cali that had the plug on many connects. Even though neither one of them needed to go back to selling illegal things they did it for the money, for their futures, for stability. Leek was running his own club and was in the process of opening a new one. Drizz and Van had a barbershop that they were getting good money from and Josiah had his moms Jamaican restaurant, and a art studio that Paige ran, and film production company. They were all heavy in clean money but it was never anything like drug money.

"Yea, she said she was going to be at the spot at 9 so if we leave at 7 shit we can make it to Napa by then.

"Alright bet. I'm up, I gotta go get Paige right quick." He slapped hands with them and got up dusting off the imaginary dirt on his pants, he walked to the door and threw up the deuce.

"I'll see yall niggas."

"Nigga make a baby." Leek joked as he closed the door.

• • ❧ • •

PAIGE OPENED THE DOOR to their townhome and was exhausted she didn't see Siah's car and knew he probably wasn't going to be home in a while. Moving her bangs out of her face before pulling the art supplies into the house she huffed. She was ecstatic and wished that Josiah was there but knew why he never came to a show. The upper echelon was never his thing. He sagged his expensive jeans, wore his gold bottoms, and his tatts made him stand out like a sore thumb. Even though she loved it to death, she hated the fact that he was so worried about messing up her image with potential buyers. She told him time and time again that she didn't give a damn about what they thought, the only thing that mattered was that he was there supporting her.

Leaning up against the door she smiled. She was hoping to lock in some sales and hopefully land some new buyers.

"I will get those sales, by the grace of God." She cheesed harder walking down the corridor into the living room. She jumped back a bit as she looked to see hundreds of red and white foil balloons.

"O shit." She smiled as she looked over and the kitchen filled to capacity with white long stemmed roses. Feeling the tears on the brim of her eyes she shook her head.

Grabbing the big card from one of the bouquet she read:

Get dressed in that dress and meet ya' nigga downtown

Smiling she took off to the room to find a silk nude pink Balmain dress with nude Louboutins. Biting her lip and shaking her head she grabbed her iPhone and took thousands of pictures and snap chats.

When daddy make you feel like a queen

And she left it at that and went to get dressed. She couldn't wait to end her night off right. Getting dressed and stepping out she saw that a strawberry pink Audi Q7, her heart dropped to her stomach and she began to cry.

"Omg this shit is so pretty." She said as she opened the door and saw a box of white chocolates, a fuzzy burgundy ball keychain and her keys. Shaking her head she smiled as she thought about all the things that he was doing.

"Ohhhh bitch is it my anniversary?" she whipped out her iPhone and checked the date. No it was far from it. It was December 20th and she smiled just knowing it was close to Christmas and her birthday. Turning the engine, she heard the engine purr as it came to life. Closing her eyes and saying a prayer she took off to her destination.

Pulling up to Morton's Steak house Paige smiled brighter than she ever had. She never understood why she was treated so well. Walking into the restaurant she was greeted by a waitress who led her to her man. Smiling as he stood up, she looked around to see that they were the only two in the room.

"Baby." Her heart fluttered with so much love.

"What?" he smiled.

"You did all this? For what?" she asked as he sat her down and she looked to see him not dressed up. That was him though, thinking of all the ways that she appreciated him, she leaned over to him and gave him a kiss on the cheek.

"Baby I missed you you should have came to my art show." She pouted as the waiter came and poured her a glass of wine.

"Shit a nigga aint tryna fuck your image up baby." He spoke pulling up his long sleeves as he drank his Hennessey."

"You could never do that baby, stop thinking that way."

Smiling and running his hands over her cheek, he kissed her.

"I love you, I have a lot of things coming up and I swear I'm a get it together, just give me time.

She nodded as they enjoyed each others time before he left her at the house and promised to come back to her before the night was over with.

• • ❧ • •

"LITE THAT SHIT." JAHARI'S smoking buddy said as she sat on her bed and lit up the blunt that was laced with coke. Jahari lit it up and hit it hard.

"Bitch see, this how a nigga treats you." The girl smiled as she scrolled down her timeline not knowing that she was scrolling on Paiges page. 3,345 likes and 500 comments. It was popping. Bringing her phone to her friend she looked at Jaharis face as she smiled and thought about how she wanted a nigga to treat her in that matter, but once she realized who it was, she was pissed and almost smashed her phone.

"Bitch I don't wanna see that bullshit, lets see how this bitch be laughing after tonight." She laughed and turned away. Her friend looked at her like she was crazy but then turned back to the pictures and screen shot some.

In the quiet town of Napa, police cars lined up to get a glimpse of the three men that they had been wanting for the past couple of years. They cleaned their acts up but now since they were making new deals, they were clean and the detectives on the case thought things went cold, until the day that received that helpful tip.

Now many squad cars lined up behind the back of the building as they prepared themselves for the exchange.

• • ❧ • •

"KITA?" PAIGE SMILED as she walked into the house with wine and in her leggings and a sweater. She could hear her talking to someone but she couldn't figure out who. Walking in closer, she could see that it was Vanilla. Rolling her eyes she kept it moving to the kitchen.

"Not today devil, not to damn day." She said loud enough for them to hear her.

"Why I gotta be a devil?" Vanilla laughed as she came into the kitchen.

"Stop."

"Nah I will not. Girl you took things the wrong way."

Taking a glass from the cabinet and shaking her head Vanilla knew how stubborn she could be, but she thought she would be ok now that she tried to explain herself.

"Uh huh sure." She poured her a glass of wine and walked out.

"So how was the date?" Kita asked as she chomped on Pizza. It was now 10 pm and they normally chilled with one another when their dudes were out handling business. Vanilla came and joined them. She was dressed to the T with her night shirt on. Turning the music on low and curling up on the couch she was ready for a girls night.

"Girl It was so nice. He took me to the steak house, we talked and enjoyed one another, then we went to the African museum, then he brought me home."

"The African museum?" Vanilla asked in disbelief. Nodding her head "Yea my baby loves cultural things."

"Wow, that's so different. So how are the paintings and shit coming? I know I want one." She told her as she grabbed the blunt wrapping papers and began to roll up.

"Yea, he's such a different man with me." she said with a twinkle in her eye. They ladies sat and discussed life, ate, watched chick flicks and curled up on the couch. They loved the days they had with each other and how they could vibe and chill with one another.

"I swear let this nigga not answer this fucking phone," I slammed onto the brakes as I swerved with Kita in the passenger side. She looked at me and shook her head. If anyone knew how me and Josiah were it was her. She knew that this nigga had my mind gone and heart open. It had been this way since I was in the 5th grade but back then I was too afraid to show it. Now here we were grown and sexy and living through some of the realest shit ever.

"But don't kill me in the process bitch," Kita said to me as I whipped the Pink G-Wagon into the driveway and rushed out. I pulled up to her house and saw that this niggas car was parked there and to say I was steaming was an understatement.

"I don't know who the fuck he thinks I am," I said to her as I power walked to the door and tried to open it but it was locked so I slammed on that hoe heavily.

Kita shook her head as she went into her purse and pulled her keys out and I chuckled a bit. I forgot she lived here. As soon as the door turned Josiah's sexy ass stepped out and looked at me. I rolled my eyes and looked down at his red bottom sneakers that I brought him as an early birthday gift last week, rag and bones jeans and black v-neck that he owned to a tee.

Fuck I loved this nigga and his deep waves helped none. I stood with my hands on my hips and he shook his head and bit his lips taking in my thick frame. My baby knew I owned this shit and his heart.

"Girl why you so fucking mad?" he questioned me and I looked away. I couldn't explain to him why I was so fucking mad. Shit he was sexy that's why. I loved his sexy ass and his hoe ass ways didn't ease my heart. Even though he swore up and down that he never fucked a bitch while I was around I knew it was a lie. A nigga will tell you the sky is purple, just to mend your heart, and a dumb ass woman will eat it up. He grabbed me into his embrace and kissed my cheek and then began to fondle the ass he couldn't stop grasping. I giggled and looked for Kita but her ass was gone.

"I called you and texted your ass," I hit his arm while he eased me back to the truck.

"I aint get shit ma," he said kissing me more and easing his hands into my pants and then unbuckled them. I looked around, it was 2 pm and he was outside trying to get some ass, the worse part was I was going to give it to him.

"Daddy stop lying," I moaned as he lifted my leg out of my jeans and spread me across the hood.

"Fuck I gotta lie for P? what daddy say about trusting him?" he said planting one finger deep in my dripping wet tunnel and then plunged into my wet walls deep, I gasped from the girth of

him. He knew I couldn't take it when he did that. I felt that shit hit my guts.

"I...I," I stuttered shit that's all I could do. He opened my legs wider and began to pound my insides out.

"Ya' nigga gets this pussy don't he?"

"Yessss," I moaned as he pinched my nipples and grinded into me.

"Then why you questioning a nigga, the way I give you dick I can't afford to have another bitch," he said closing his eyes as I clamped my pussy muscles down on him.

I don't know why I questioned my man, maybe because we were too perfect. After a minute he nutted off in me and then pulled me in close for a kiss. One thing I had to say about Josiah is that he didn't give a fuck who was watching, when he wanted his kitten to purr he made that hoe meow. Fixing me up and smacking my ass he shook he head as I tried to switch in the house.

"You know damn well this dick can't have you walking normal, you still aint used to it," he said and I laughed. He was right though. I looked at him and loved the man that he was. He took me on extravagant trips, nightly chef made dinners, I got whatever I needed and didn't need shit else. I guess I just needed to trust in my man.

"I love you Paige," he said to me in a genuine tone and it touched my heart.

"I love you more," I blew him a kiss and watched him walk to his car, a black with white interior 1979 mustang and roll the windows down.

"Dinner at 8 baby?" I nodded

Waking up from her vivid dream she jumped up and expected to feel Siahs arms wrapped around her. Nothing yet, she turned back around and as the hours went by and the ladies were asleep cuddled up to pillows and blankets. Feeling the need to look at her phone she realized it was dead. It was 5 am and she was wondering where her man was. Looking outside she didn't see anything or anyone.

Sighing she checked on Vanilla and Kita they were knocked out.

"Kita?" she asked before she heard her phone ringing. Rushing to it she looked at the unknown number.

"Hello?"

"Baby I fucked up." She heard Josiah say on the other end.

"What?" her heart dropped as she felt like her world was coming to an end.

"Baby I need you to come down here fast, get some money from my momma and bail me out."

"Where are you Josiah?"

"I'm locked up on a bullshit ass charge."

"What charge?"

"Intent to sale and buy and some more shit."

Feeling her temper about to spiral out of control she saved it.

"Where are you?"

"I'm in Napa." Closing her eyes she wanted to scream. She didn't know which way to go. She couldn't lose him at a time like this, not now. Shaking her head and deciding to pull herself together she hung up with him, woke up the girls and went to get his mom.

Within hours the police department was loaded with women who cared about their men. Concerned faces were everywhere. She waited as everyone piled out of the rooms everyone except for Josiah. Once she saw his lawyer she and his mother stood.

"What's going on?" she asked as they left the police department.

"They are holding him on higher charges than everyone else. Her heart fell.

"We have to wait until the bond hearing."

Turning to Shantriece he held her hand and then held Paige's.

"He said he will call tonight and he loves you both." She nodded at the sound of that and as soon as the lawyer walked off she broke down crying. Shantriece walked to her and held her up. Looking into her eyes she shook her head.

"You stay strong yuh 'ere me?" he thick Jamaican accent coming out.

"Ghana doesn't do weak, and your no weak gyal, now I'm a go home. I want you to bring all the valubles you guys own to my house. I don't know what they will do but you bring it all to me. I own my house and I have the money to show how. So make sure you do it tonight and hurry."

She said in final as she walked off and left Paige standing there to be strong. Looking at Vanilla and Kita they surrounded her with love and hugs and all she could think of was being strong.

It took her 3 hours to clean out her safe, his clothes, his shoes and more things and stash them in the bottom of his mother's house. By the time she was done everyone was sitting waiting for him to call. The call never came.

The next morning, they all woke up and went to the bond hearing. The judge didn't give him a bond due to the severity of the case. As much as he looked like he wanted to pop he stayed calm and collected. Looking back at his girl and his mom he smiled as they took him off to jail. The court process went on for about 2 months and with in those months Paige was fighting with her all to get him out and to get her families house. Everything was finally looking up until the day that the judge sentenced Josiah.

Looking around she saw a familiar face. It was Jahari sitting there with sunglasses on. There was no way she was going to miss this. Looking at her she winked.

"Ghana-Keyair "Josiah" Foster," the judge said as he looked at the paper before him.

"We sentence you to 7 years in prison." Her heart sped up and she looked back at Jahari who was clapping while walking out. Shaking her head, she didn't want to believe what was happening. Everything was happening so fast. Walking over to him before they pulled him out, she grabbed Josiah and kissed his lips.

"Baby I'm a call you later ok?" he told her and she nodded.

"I love you baby." She cried out and he nodded.

Looking at his mom, he turned to walk off. The lawyer looked at her and shook his head at the situation.

"You know that lady that was clapping?" he told her. She nodded.

"She was the one that made the statement and the drop." He whispered and she took off running in search of her evil ass sister. Once outside she saw Jahari get into the car with someone that looked familiar.

"Daryl?" she asked as she passed out on the steps.

Thank you for supporting me.. I swear no more short stories, no more no more. I have many books and sequels for you all this new year, 2016 is looking great. Thank you all for the support. Please join my mailing list by sending me an email to lolabandzz@gmail.com

This is a novella. Look for the extended version when they join Xaylin, Raziyah (From the holiday story), and Josiah and Paige in:

"Me & My G" February 2016

Enjoy this from Author Aaleyah:

Get Ya' Money..

Now Available

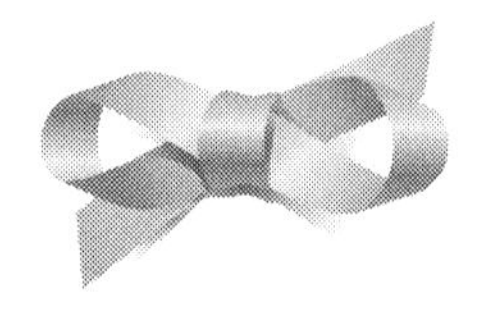

Prologue

May 23,2010. 12:25AM.
Golden Temptation Strip Club

Cleopatra

When I stepped off the bus it was dark but the hot air immediately greeted me with a hello. I reached into my black, over-the-shoulder purse to still find the heap of money safely stashed away. Just the feel of it gives me hope. *"A fresh start,"* I thought to myself as I reminisced what happened the previous week.

Graduating from high-school is no easy job. There's always distractions and temptations around every corner. You had to be strong to make it through and I did. So here I am in sunny Sacramento, California, a whole different state, environment and people. I came a long way from Brick, New Jersey and an even longer way from Nigeria.

• • ∞ • •

Now I've been walking for hours. My feet were cramping, my back hurts and I'm sweating because

I was dressed like an Eskimo when it's clearly about 100 degrees out here. Not to mention, I'm exhausted. I came upon a black building with golden trimmings and a golden shape lady dancing in heels. *"It has to be a strip club,"* I thought.

I heard fast paced music booming and a voice saying, "Work that monkey." I rolled my eyes. Whatever that is. I stopped near the entrance to look in when a red-bone chick with loud red hair came out talking loud and yelling on her phone. She looked at me weird and proceeded to her Benz. I was lost and at least needed a hotel to stay in.

"Aye!" I looked to see the red-headed chick waving me over as I walked over to the driver's side where she was.

"Yeah?" I asked.

"You look lost and by what you wearing I could tell you ain't from round he'ya are ya?" She asked. I could tell she was from down south because her county accent was too heavy not to be.

"Nah." I said, my Nigerian accent waving heavily.

"Wh'ea ya from?" She asked noticing my unfamiliar accent.

"Nigeria but I moved to Brick, New Jersey when I was two." I said.

"New Jersey?" She asked eyes widened.

"Yep." I said smiling.

"Me too!" She yelled getting excited.

"Cool." I said smiling.

"I'm Kandice but folks round che'ya call me Lil Red." Kandice said moving her curly waist length hair from her face.

"I'm Cleopatra but people call me Cleo." I said.

"Aye nice, like the Egyptian Queen?" Kandice asked tooting her nose up.

I laughed." Yea like her." I said while nodding my head. She welcomed me into her car so I walked over to the passenger side.

"Aye Kandice, do you know where I can get a hotel at?" I asked shifting my seat to get comfortable.

"Sure do but there's no need." Kandice said starting the car. I gripped the blade I had in my jacket pocket.

"Why?" I asked getting kind of tensed. I guess she could tell it because she busted out laughing and hitting me playfully on the arm.

"Girl, chill. I ain't finna kidnap you. I'm crazy, not stupid. I am just inviting you to my crib." Kandice said.

"Really?" I asked not believing what I just heard.

"Yes girl." Kandice said smiling friendly.

"Thank you." I said smiling back.

It was quiet. Only the music was vibing through the car as she drove and I rode..

"Yo, you think Cleopatra was a sista?" Kandice asked.

"Girl ain't no telling. Her paternal grandmother was Nubian which is considered as Black today and her mother was Semitic African. So yeah, she was a sista." I said.

"Look at you all smart and stuff." Kandice said laughing.

• • ❧ • •

"Kandice do you have some shorts a little longer?" I asked looking at myself in the full body mirror in her bathroom.

"Cleopatra it looks fine!" Kandice said.

"I'm not coming out!" I protested sitting on the brown square tiles. I heard Kandice laugh.

"Suit yo'rs." She called.

After ten minutes I came out and she was right there in the living room watching television. I slowly crept out and Kandice laughed once more.

"I can see yo'r gonna be extra girl."

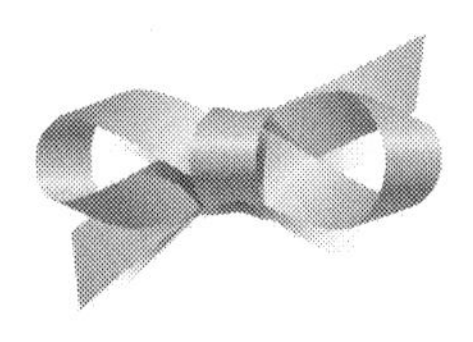

Chapter 1: Get Ready
3 Years Later...
July 4th,2013, 11:23am
Cleo's Crib.

Cleopatra

I squinted my eyes and moaned from the tapping California sunlight against my face. Thoughts instantly bit at my brain of my birthday bash. Tonight fya girl turning the big 21 y'all! I'm too excited! Finally I'll be old enough to get into the club. Yessss! I don't know what ol' crazy Kandice got in store because she's the type of friend that goes all out. She will buy you an elephant and say Happy Birthday just to say she did it; you just never know with her. Good thing I scheduled off from work. Shoot, I did that two weeks prior. Oh before I forget, yes I am a baby that was painted with my red, white and blue stripes at birth. Shout-out to all the Independence Day babies out there.

My phone was singing out sweet melodies by my baby Jacquees. *Me, U and Hennessy* filled the air indicating that I had text messages and social media notifications. I clicked on my messages. There were three from my migga, jigga nigga Kandice, one from my brother Josh and a few more from other people. Then I went to my Instagram and my notifications were on fye. I had 1,000 happy birthday shout-outs and one was from nobody other than Messiah!

I read it out loud to myself. *@Qveen_Cleopatra Happy 21st birthday bby girl. I can not believe we went so long without seeing each other. I remember you was the quiet girl in the back of the class with braces and binoculars. Lol look at chu, a beautiful woman!! I hope you enjoy it, and in fact, I know you will. I'll be seeing you beautiful! <3 P.S. you will always be my little nerd. :).*

OH MY FREAKING GOSH! Messiah! I haven't seen him in ages. I had a mega-crush on him ever since we were shorties on the sidewalk eating seeds and pickles together. I remember the first day we had officially met.

His Brown Skin Drug
Diamond Dior
Coming Soon...
Lisa

"Come Thru-o-o-o," I sang rolling my hips along with the tune coming from the radio in the diner.

"Shit this my jam, I'm a do a dance to this Nini," I enthused as I bit my lips, moving my hips behind the counter eyeing Nia.

"Girl go clean table three before Mr. Dean see you out here dancing when you should be working," Nia nagged shaking her head, her supposedly white apron had a brown stains splattered on the front as if she was rolling in mud, her hands were filled with a mountain of dirty dishes. She's a beautiful girl; she has big, bright, brown eyes that held in a spark that was irresistible to look at. Her complexion was the color of a perfectly created Hershey chocolate bar. She always wore a smile that brightened anyone's day. Her short baby looking curly hair is cut in a bob which complemented her entire facial feature. We stood the same height of 5'10 feet. Despite her attire now she was still beautiful.

"Ugh, fine, always gotta kill my vibes" I stopped playing around to attend to the customers.

My parents named me as Lisa Chin, but my friends call me Lee. I'm 24 and single with no kids. I share an apartment in New York with my best friend Nia and we work together at Diner 24/7. Working at the diner is just a hobby; I come from a wealthy family. Being the only child my 'dad' and 'mom' still gives me money even when I tell them not to. They adopted me when I was 1 year old, my mother died at childbirth and my father is nowhere to be found. I have a great passion for dancing, that is my only talent, I love it, I graduated from college with bachelors in fine arts. Yes a qualified dancer.

I have a light brown complexion that resembles smooth caramel and I have a pair of deceiving hazel eyes that has got me in trouble on many occasions. I was blessed with long natural hair which I have no intention of perming. I straighten it when I'm ready or I leave it curly as it is. Right now I have it straightened with bleached extensions at the ends; I think bleaching my actual hair will damage it. I have a beauty mark on the right side of my face right under my cheek which complimented my complexion. I was told by the adoption agency that my mother was a beautiful girl. I would like to believe that I got my beauty from her.

"Girl come give yo' man a kiss" came a semi bass voice from the entrance of the diner.

"James get your crusty ass out the diner if you come in here to start shit with your perv ass" I joked and cut my eyes at him playfully.

He always gotta come in here trying to talk to me or Nia but he was never serious. He just wants to get us heated and he knows nobody wants his dead beat ass, he got about a dozen kids and he keeps running from his baby mamas. It is said on the streets that he has a little brother who's a big time drug dealer in California.

"Lisa baby come sit in daddy's lap and tell him why you sound so upset," he cooed and smiled, sliding in a booth which was occupied by a lady drinking her coffee.

"Sorry babe I didn't see you there, you mind me joining you?" he smirked as if he was slick.

"Actually yes, my husband is on his way, please get up!" she said sternly, your ass just got checked!

"Ha! She wants me," he smirked sliding into an empty booth

"If only you were good looking," I responded and shook my head.

"What's that suppose to mean?" he answered, his smile set on reverse.

"James, what do you want?" I asked quickly as I took out my notepad and pen.

"Can I get grilled chicken sandwich with cheese, a beer and on the side, a piece of you." he answered and winked, running his tongue against his lower lip causing a disgusted chill to run through my body.

"Yes, Yes and No." I snapped before I rolled my eyes and walked off towards the counter.

"Ugh! Here." I dropped the order on the counter.

"Lemme' guess your husbands is here isn't he." she smirked referring to James as she turned around to give the chef the order.

"He is not my man and yes." I responded and gave her a straight face.

"I'm just kidding girl, you going dancing tonight?" she asked with giggle at my reaction.

"Yes! I have to, there is this club named Beat Box. I wanna hit it up tonight."

"Hmm what am I gonna wear though?" she thought out loud as she pouted, passing me James order

"Girl you got my closet, we tight." I winked walking off.

"Here you go James." I scoffed as I placed his order on the table.

"Thanks babe." He said with a smirk snug on his face.

"James how comes you look so decent today?" I asked in almost mocking tone.

"My lil' brother is coming from Cali today and we gon' hang out, why you wanna' come?"

"No thanks." I walked off. What I look like going out with him?

THE MOMENT I WALKED into the apartment I released a sigh filled with weariness and stress. I allowed my feet to guide me as my toes swam through the crème carpet that flooded the entire apartment. My sore feet led me to my mini heaven on earth. My sofa; made of the softest suede found in Ashley's' Store in town. I allowed the softness of the sofa to pull me into a daze of relaxation.

"Damn I need a shower." I moaned rolling over onto my back.

"Go get one and get your sweaty ass out the couch." Nia teased and pushed me off the couch.

I got up and dragged myself towards my bedroom to have a shower. As I opened the door to my personal kingdom, I was greeted with a strong feminine scent which means my Pink Friday perfume was still in the air. I dropped my handbag at my door and used my leg to close the door that shut with a small click. As I headed for the bathroom, I turned on my 32" all black, flat screen, Samsung Smart television that sat on my crème wall to BET since it was my favorite channel since I was a teen. The entire apartment is in crème and burgundy. I think it made the penthouse apartment feel more homely and it just flowed better together.

"Welcome back to 106 & Park this is your girl Rosci! and here is number four on the charts, 'She' by Keisha Cole." Rosci voice faded as soon as I closed the bathroom door.

I stripped myself of my grease filled uniform and threw them in my dirty clothes hamper. I turned on the shower and gauged it then let it run for a while I fetched my bottle of Dove body wash and climbed over into my mini spa. The warm water slowly opened my pores allowing the stress and weariness to ooze out. Lathering my skin with Dove, I moaned as I felt the relaxation come over me like a wave.

"Damn I need a man."

I washed off and stepped out the shower before I grabbed my pink towel that sat neatly on the silver rack opposite to the shower.

Wrapping my towel around me I tucked the end above my breast and walked over to my now fogged mirror. I used my right index finger to make a smiley face in the fog. I can be so childish at times. I shook my head, walking out the bathroom.

My warm body was smacked with a cool air as soon as I opened the door. Strolling over to my walking closet, I mentally choose the outfit I wanted to wear tonight. I pulled out a black thigh dress with a pair of silver sandals; trying not to overdo myself. I applied a little makeup; Mascara, eyeliner, eye shadow and lipstick. I grabbed my silver clutch and left with Nia to the club.

"COME THRU, GIRL YOU know we got things to do," I sang purposely off key, grinding my hips in the passenger seat as Nia drove my car; I was not in the mood to drive tonight.

"Man, I am feeling this album, one of greatest shit Drake ever did." I enthused and rocked to the song.

"Lee why don't you start your own dancing classes. I mean you went to college, you got your stuff, why don't you teach people to dance, because I see you and you're great." Nia asked, stopping at the stop light. I watched the red light turn green feeling the car moving again.

"Girl, you know that ain't true." I retorted and smacked my lips, running my fingers through my hair.

"Whatever." she muttered and parked at a curb, one four blocks from the club, and we got out. Being that its Friday night It would be packed tonight, so we have to park far so that we won't have to encounter any problems when we're ready to leave.

"Shit, he's the bouncer tonight, Lee he's yours." Nia whispered and hissed her teeth. *This bitch always have me doing the most.*

Fixing my dress, I held my clutch in hand and walked up to the bouncer with a seductive demeanor.

"Hey sexy," I was greeted by his well painted yellow teeth as he grinned down at me, his eyebrows in a wiggling motion and he fixed his black tuxedo. The sight of him made my stomach churn. His big, broad shoulders that kept his big head upright blocked me from seeing inside.

"Hey what's up?" I purred and batted my long

"You're looking good in that dress." He commented and ran his tongue against his crusty looking lower lip. I cleared my throat so that he wouldn't hear me gag in my mouth."Thanks." I continued purring with a forced smile on my face.

"Wanna give me your number?" he asked eyeing me with a smirk now settled on his face.

"Sure!" I fakely enthused and I quickly wrote down a fake number on his hand and with that, he slipped us in the club.

"Took his ass so long," Nia complained and sighed.

"I got my eyes on you

You're everything that I see

I want your hot love and emotion Endlessly..." came Drake's music blasting from all corners of the club.

"Damn, drake everywhere." I mumbled as Nia pulled me to the dance floor. We danced together, grinding and rolling our curves that were in the right places, getting stares from a lot of people; mostly guys. Some of the guys even tried to pry us apart for a one on one dance but we were inseparable on the dancefloor.

After the dancing, we walked to the bar and ordered us both a bottle of Myx fusion, then we headed to the back to a table for two.

"This club is packed" Nia shouted over the music and took a sip of her drink, nodding her head to the music.

"Yeah" I answered and looked around when suddenly, my eyes landed on this group of men, all dressed in black, but there was one particular guy in the group that caught my eyes.

He was the only one in the group wearing gold for the color of his accessories; his wristwatch and earring. The others were in silver accessories. I was mesmerized by his facial features; I couldn't see his eyes that much but they were low, he was laughing with the guys and I saw a dimple, he was dark brown and his looked buffed; damn he was looking right, not to mention his lips they looked soft and luscious. One of his men whispered in his ears and slowly I saw him turn around and stare at me while he ran his tongue over his lower lip in a timely manner. I broke the stare and turned back around to Nia.

"Is he still looking at me?" I asked as I hung my head down after taking a sip of my drink.

"Who?" She asked chirpily as she looked around.

"No! Stop, behind me, full black, only one wearing gold" I responded quickly, the blood rushing to my cheeks.

"Shit he must be good looking if he got you blushing" she teased and sneakily looked over my shoulder "Yup he is looking good"

"He's handsome isn't he?" I asked biting my lower lip

"Yes girl and he is on his way over here"

"What?!?" I gasped and desperately tried fixing my hair "How do I look?" I asked Nia in a rushed way.

"Fine, damn fine. Come dance with me for a minute Ma."" Came a bass voice whisper from behind me and then I felt his warm breathe against my earlobe.

The chills that ran up my spine had me pressing my thighs together. *Who was this nigga?*

I looked up at Nia "Go," she mouthed to me with a sneaky grin.

"Okay." I agreed and with that he lead me to the dance floor. A slow song was being played and so we swayed gently to the music.

"I saw you looking at me." He whispered in my neck, sending a chill down my spine. This one was a one I enjoyed running down my spine and into my body.

"I saw you looking at me too" I whispered back "Don't even ask me if I liked what I saw because men these days are getting cocky off natural air" I joked and rested my head on his chest a bit. His cologne had me in a daze.

"I wasn't going to ask, it's obvious you did." I felt the shift of his lips on my head; he smirked then turning me around so that my back was facing his chest.

"Now we gon' hit the Nineties baby!" the DJ scratched the track and flipped it over,

then "This Is How We Do It" by Montel Jordan came on and we started to bounce on each other like they did back in the nineties.

"Let's get a drink" he suggested after our nineties dancing took a toll on our stamina. he showed me to the bar "what do you want ma'?"

"Water" I told him, taking in deep breaths

"Water?" he asked as he raised eyebrows.

"Yeah, I had a little too much Myx for the night" she admits with a slight giggle.

"Aight I got you ma," He smiled then turned to the bartender "let me get a bottle of Ciroc and a bottle of water for the lady."

"Here you go" he said and handed me my water as soon as he got it.

"Than-" I began but was interrupted by a loud yell.

"Shotta yuh a guh dead!" a voice with an unusual accent shouted over the music followed by an array of gun shots.

"Ahh!!!" I screamed dropping my water and my body practically went into shock. I couldn't move. He had to drag me out through the back door after firing what sounded like four shots.

I tried breathing slowly but I couldn't. I was still in shock and all that replayed were the gun shots in my head. His hands fumbled as he unlocked and opened in his sleek, black BMW

"Get in the car ma' or else you gon' get hurt." He warned in a rush from the driver seat.

“No, you knew damn well shit would pop off didn’t you?” I shouted crossing my hands.

“Just get in the fucking car!”

“No!” I walked back to the back door. “I’m not leaving with you.”

“Yes you are!” I felt my body being lift off the ground.

“Ah!” I screamed as I kicked fighting for my life. “Help! Ah let me the fuck go!”

“Shut up!” He growled as he placed me in the passenger seat then quickly buckled the seat belt.

Click! Click! He slipped the child lock on then locked the door.

Soon he got in and put the car in reverse but that didn't go as plan due to the man than ran through the back door we came through.

"Fuck!" He cursed as he put the car in drive.

As we sped off gun shots fired at the back of the car as I screamed.

"Ahhhh!!!" I was scared as hell who the fuck was this nigga?

"Shit." He hissed.

His voice brought me back to reality for a second and I took a look around carefully. Why the hell would he park his car at the back unless he knew that shit would blow!

"Who the fuck are you? Why did you do that? Why are people after you? And Why do you have a gun?" I was beyond confused. *Damn I always get my ass tangled in some shit I don't belong in.*

"What is your name?" I asked confused and dazed while I stared blankly at him trying to cover up the fear that ran through me.

"Answer me now!" I shouted.

The car came to a halt and I looked around to see the car surrounded by darkness. *Fuck it I was one dead bitch, he was going to kill me. Nini always said my mouth would get my ass in trouble one of these days.*

He stared at me blankly with his killer eyes, it was like he could see through me; I could tell by his demeanor, he wasn't fazed. He was a pro at reading people.

Looking down at my fingers tears pooled up at the lids of my eyes ready to pour.

He started the car again and pulled out of the back parking lot and headed to the highway.

"You hungry ma'?" he asked and ran his hand over his face then leaned back in his seat relaxed.

Relaxed?! I know damn well this nigga wasn't being relaxed after what just happened.

"Amaree."

Looking up I looked at him.

"My name is Amaree."

"Lisa." I looked at him biting my lower lip.

"Because you crying you looked fuck up right about now I wouldn't advice you to bite you lower lips ma'." He shut me down.

"So are you hungry ma'?" he asked again. *Talk about persistent.*

"Shit!" I exclaimed as I came to a realization.

"Everything alright?" He asked glancing behind him to look at me.

"I left my clutch with my phone at the table with Nia ... NIA! fuck! I left her." I exclaimed and stuck my hand into my hair and dragged it down my face, resting my face in my palms.

"Shit, don't cry, use my phone and call her." He suggested and gave me his phone as he approached Burger Kings drive thru.

I called her quickly, making a few mistakes as I dialed her number. I cursed under my breath but I finally got to dial and she said she is okay and is on her way home. I told her that I was okay and I would be home soon, only because Amaree was listening.

"She okay?" He asked as I returned his phone and turned the car off, that's when I realized that we were parked in front a beach

"Yeah" I replied and returned his phone with a sigh.

"Here I got you some nuggets and fries." He told me and handed me the box.

Execution food. My last meal. I thought as I accepted the box.

"Thanks" I muttered.

"If was going to kill you ma' you would have been dead before we left the club. If I left you there you would have been dead."

"Why?"

"Because of who I am."

"Who are you Amaree?" My curiosity got the best of me and soon I craved knowing more. I wanted to know him.

"I'm someone you shouldn't fuck with ma'." He said stuffing his mouth with fries.

SOMEHOW I FELT SAFE around him. I know I just met him, but the more I got to know him the more intoxicating he became to me; like he wouldn't harm a fly though he would do more than that.

"I guess I don't have to explain to you who or what I am to you since you saw what happened tonight." He mumbled and looked at me in my seat that was placed back so I can lay down since I was tired.

Yes, he was one dangerous nigga.

"No, it was pretty clear to me who and what you are, it's just that I don't know everything." I responded and turned on my side, getting comfortable and ready for him to share his story with me.

"After tonight your life won't be the same ma'. People will be after you to kill you to reach to me."

"all you did was take me out the club with you." I chuckled.

"I don't ever do shit for people, you in a mess you stay in that shit and figure a way out yourself."

"Saving me made them think we are close."

"I'm never close to anyone."

"We can go to the police about this right."

"Police." He chuckled.

"If they caught me they would execute you."

That's when my heart dropped. *Round of applause Lisa you done got yo' ass in some deep shit this time.*

"What?" I gulped as knots tangled in my stomach.

"After tonight disappear, go somewhere Mexico." He said so calmly. *This was nothing new to him.*

"No." I eased up and stared at him.

"What?"

"I said *No* I will not leave."

"You aren't meant for this life we can not be around each other."

"Its my choice I want us to be friends."

"Friends." He scoffed. "Your trying to commit suicide forget it ma.""

"The child's lock."

"What about it?"

"It clicked twice." I folded my arms pushing up my boobs. It was a habit I had when I was about to prove a point.

"So?"

Pulling the handle on the door it opened. "...So it's not closed, you weren't planning to hurt me, you said it yourself if you were going to kill me you would have done it already."

He stared into my eyes with a spark in his a smirk curved on his face an soon a dimple was on his left cheek. *Damn.*

"Now that we are friends tell me about you." I stared at him smirking. *Damn I was sweating bullets with my brave ass.*

I watched as he laid back in his seat sighing with his hands behind his head and his eyes closed.

"You little bitch." I hissed my teeth. *I could a see where we be arguing already.*

"I am not an American, I am from Jamaica. My father brought me up here when I was six to live with my mother and my older brother. My older brother wasn't my father's child and we found out while we live in Cali. My father disappeared after five months after he got my mother pregnant again and she was getting worried and shit. My brother was done with all the shit that was happening so he moved out here in New York and she couldn't do shit on her own so I started selling. Just like my mama I was loyal; to my gang and family I worked and did what I was told never once did a nigga steal. Before I knew it I was my boss right hand. He got aids and died. He was my only father figure in and out the streets, I was damaged when he died. In his will he left a nigga everything he worked for, now I'm the Cartel for the east side of Cali. Now my momma and my lil' sister are treated like royalties" He explained to me, gazing at the stars. And to think he was just a seller when he is actually a king pin.

What the fuck did I get myself into, a drug cartel. My father is a police of the fucking state!

"Wow. You don't sound Jamaican though" I commented and yawned as my eyes fluttered... "So what about your brother, is he still in New York?" I asked and looked over at him.

"I had to adapt to my society ma', Niggas crossed my turf, a couple died and I had to pay my respects today, today was they funeral and my bro still here we hanged out today and shit."

"Damn I got an headache." I mumbled.

"Here some aspirin for that ma'."

"You keep asprin in your car?"

"Something like that."

"Okay, your so mysterious." I giggled throwing the pills in my mouth. The moment I swallow them I heard my heartbeat in my ears and soon my vision became blurry.

"Ama-"

Don't miss out!

Click the button below and you can sign up to receive emails whenever Lola Bandz publishes a new book. There's no charge and no obligation.

https://books2read.com/r/B-A-JDRB-ANZH

Connecting independent readers to independent writers.

Did you love *A Hood Luv Tale*? Then you should read *Dreams of F**** A D-Boy* by Lola Bandz and Diamond DIor!

Lanika and Aaliyah are sisters that are trying to pave their way in the world after their parents death. Lanika being the oldest takes care of her little sister by doing the only thing she knows, dating a D-Boy. Not knowing that the relationship seems perfect, but all that glitters isnt gold, and thats something that Aaliyah finds out the hard way when she starts dating a D-Boy.

Aaliyah thinks that the fast life is the best life, losing her parents and depending on her sister for the love and support she needs, she falls into the arms of Prince, one ot the local D-Boys, but will Prince show her that D-Boys are a dream or a headache?

Find Out in this gritty urban drama "Dreams Of Fucking A D-Boy." by Diamond Dior & Lola Bandz

Also by Lola Bandz

Deranged Loverz
Deranged Loverz

Dopeboys
Dreams of F**** A D-Boy

Killa Gram
Killa Gram: Kilos come up

Kilos Cocaine
Kilos Cocaine 3

Standalone
Kilos Cocaine

Fyast Life
Kilos Cocaine 2
A Hood Luv Tale
My Old Freak
Luvin A Thug
Bad 4 You

About the Author

Lola Bandz, is well known for her swagged out thug books, that empower women, and leave your jaw dropped. Growing up in the bay area played a great deal to her style. She brings back the urban, street lit classics, and makes sure that they remain fresh, new, and dope.

Read more at www.dopegirlzink.com.

About the Publisher

A company where we strive to bring the heat back to the game.

Made in the USA
Columbia, SC
21 July 2024

39122243R00074